BOLD SPIRIT

BOLD SPIRIT

Wallis Peel

CHIVERS

British Library Cataloguing in Publication Data available

This Large Print edition published by BBC Audiobooks Ltd, Bath, 2007.
Published by arrangement with the Author.

U.K. Hardcover ISBN 978 1 405 64162 3
U.K. Softcover ISBN 978 1 405 64163 0

20174445

Printed and bound in Great Britain by
Antony Rowe Ltd., Chippenham, Wiltshire

For Viv Nichol

ONE

Anne Howard tossed her mane of light brown hair aside, and took another deep breath as she lifted her head from the floorboards. At this point, the floor rushes were old, and so their voices had been clear. The Will's reading showed her old master had been worth the stupendous sum of thirty-two pounds ten shillings and sixpence farthing and his heir was his odious nephew

There was silence now from below, and she guessed the men were drinking ale so she thought quietly and rapidly. Through the half-opened shutters she could smell the countryside, but her mind was too troubled now to appreciate the odours of grasses, leaves and general farm smells.

She tiptoed from the room and climbed the bare wooden stairs to her attic and sank down miserably on the truckle bed with its thin, straw mattress. Anne stared unhappily at the bare boards, splintered in a few places, while trepidation filled her. Jacob Selwell had been her master and, at times, a harsh one, but there had been something reassuring about his presence. His unexpected death, and this news of his nephew's inheritance was ghastly. She shivered. Because of her master's childless state, that nephew had visited often and Anne had loathed his ogling eyes which stripped her naked with promised intent.

Outside, the sun shone brilliantly, and later the cows would require milking. She studied her hands ruefully. They were large, capable and calloused. The skin always split and chapped in the cold months, while in the summer it was leathery and dry, despite applications of goose grease. Her fingers were wide, strong and well-developed, and now she clenched them into fists.

Anne's mind raced as she struggled to assemble known facts into a coherent sequence of understanding, because she had known nothing but this farm. She had been told she was born a foundling seventeen years ago, and Jacob Selwell had taken her in, given her a home and reared her out of Christian charity. It was true, he had fed and clothed her, even given her some book learning but, on the reverse side, he had also given her plenty of hidings when the fit took him.

Anne frowned. As a small child, Jacob had terrified her but, as she grew, she acquired a wary respect for him. Once or twice, she had felt this was reciprocated but these occasions were fleeting because it took little for Jacob's gaze to return to its usual cold, narrow-eyed glower.

Perhaps if Jacob's wife Mary had lived, there might have been a better atmosphere. As it was, Mary's widowed cousin Agnes became

Jacob's housekeeper on her death and, Anne knew, Agnes disliked her intensely for some reason. There were days when Anne was a bundle of twitching nerves, never sure when Agnes would not shout at or hit her.

Most masters considered their young female employees fair bed game as Anne knew, yet Jacob had never approached her, which puzzled and irked. She thought she knew why. The pond's waters had shown she had regular features, though they lacked beauty. Anne considered her long, fine hair to be her outstanding attribute. She could not see her large, frank eyes—an odd blue-grey, which changed with her moods—hinting at a spirit not yet free.

There were few jobs on the farm she could not tackle but, early on, Jacob had discovered she had a natural affinity with animals. Her domestic work came to an end when he put her outside. The cows never fussed about letting down their milk. No hen pecked when she took an egg, and the rooster's aggression was more bluff than action. The pigs considered her a friend, and even the ram had never more than half-heartedly butted her. With horses this affinity became a gift.

The outdoor work made her grow tall, big-boned and strong, while disease missed her. She ate well, at the communal table, because Jacob's appetite was hearty, and he was not mean with the food he provided for his servants. That this made a hard life, seven days a week, had never entered Anne's head, simply because she knew no better for her menial class.

She had no friend, but felt no lack. She had a fair idea of who was whom in the village's hierarchy—the most important of who was old Lady Sarah Penford, who lived alone in rich, stately splendour about a mile away. On the far side of the village was another female Penford, with the reputation of a quarrelsome, acid tongue. These well-off people derived their income from trade in Bristol, although the village itself was agrarian.

Anne's confused thoughts slid to the Hiring Fair, which would be held soon. Did she have the courage to put herself up for bidding? Certainly she did not fancy staying in her present position, with a hostile Agnes, and the lecherous new owner.

With a sigh she stood, smoothed the thin, grey, cotton gown over which was tied a long white apron. Once again, she wondered if she dared to ask Agnes. Because never far from the forefront of her mind was the perennial question who were her parents? From where did she come? She ran her tongue over her bottom lip indecisively because decisions had always been made by Jacob. The effort of making a plan was daunting yet also tantalisingly attractive.

She had no idea she was the chrysalis that

had lain dormant for months, but was now ready to stir for its natural metamorphosis. She dithered a few more moments with conflicting emotions. Then made up her mind. It all depended upon what mood Agnes was in.

Anne went down the wooden stairs, resolution growing. Perhaps if she could learn her breeding, she might receive a pointer as to whether she should parade at the Hiring Fair. She paused and her willpower deserted, her heart sank. Agnes was clattering pans and muttering under her breath. She opened the door and saw the thundercloud on the older woman's red face.

'So there you are,' Agnes snapped. 'You come over here and help me with all this washing-up. I can't be expected to do everything myself with those men wanting drink and food. It's high time there were alterations in this house, and I'll be seeing the new Master about long overdue changes, I can tell you!' she continued grimly, breasts heaving wrathfully. Black hair, laced with grey, had come a little untwined from a thick bun as she banged a sooty iron cauldron down on the fire's trivet, put hands on her ample hips and glowered at the younger girl.

'It's time you earned your keep here, working for me, not spending all day gadding about with the animals. It's not decent. Especially the way the old master taught you to ride like a man,' she accused.

Anne felt herself blush. Why Jacob had taken it into his head to do this had puzzled her as well but she had never dared to question his motives. Her thirst for knowledge made her an avid pupil and a natural seat with delicate hands had demonstrated a rapport with horses. It was true her master would bellow at her mistakes and no word of praise ever left his lips, though sometimes, she had fancied, his eyes glowed with delight.

'What do you mean, Agnes?' she managed to get out nervously.

'The new master won't hold with fanciful ideas. Your place will be here in the kitchen until you are wed. A boy is going to see to the animals.' Agnes paused and ran her eye over the girl facing her. 'Girls of your age are long wed, with one at the breast, and another on the way.' She paused with narrow eyes. 'The new master won't stand any nonsense from you either.'

Anne stared back, appalled at this and the first stir of revolt thrust up its head. Life would be a misery, working under Agnes and a wave of panic flared.

'I'll not be married just because!' she shot back swiftly.

Agnes halted with a shock, hardly able to believe her ears. She strode forward two paces over the stone-flagged floor and faced Anne, her brown eyes blazing in shock and anger. 'You will do as you are told,' she shouted. 'You will be lucky to get a man anyhow with your background!'

Anne blinked and furrowed her forehead. 'What do you mean, Agnes?'

The older woman snorted in disbelief. 'Don't act the innocent with me. You know perfectly well, you were Jacob Selwell's by-blow from that whore Emma Howard!'

Anne was aghast at this revelation. 'I did not!' she protested while her mind buzzed with implications. Quite suddenly, many small pieces of a complex jigsaw slid into place. Jacob's willingness to give her some education. The way he had taught her to ride and allowed her free rein with the animals. The times when his eyes displayed something more than their usual coolness. At the time, she had taken these to be a master's quirkiness. It also explained why he had never attempted to bed her. Indeed, she recollected how, when any casual labourer cast sheep's eyes at her, Jacob had always glowered.

'But if he was—' she began uncertainly.

'Of course he was!' Agnes interrupted. 'And nearly broke his poor wife's heart when her babies died. When he installed you here, raised you, then gave you free rein, my cousin turned to the bedroom wall and gave up. Her death was all your fault!' Agnes snapped bitterly.

'Rubbish!' Anne retorted hotly. 'That wasn't my doing!' She swallowed at her blatant cheek, while Agnes's face went redder. 'I had no idea. He never said a word to me.'

Agnes snorted. 'Maybe not, but I knew, and so did others. And don't you dare use that tone of voice with me either, you young hussy!'

Anne was speechless and turned this over with a sinking heart. She felt a sharp sadness. If only Jacob had told her but then, she argued, what good would this revelation have done?

'You'll see. The new master has changes in mind. I've already had a talk with him about you!' Agnes said triumphantly. The sooner this hussy was brought to order, the better for all concerned. Her dear cousin's heart had broken with a daily reminder of her husband's infidelity.

Anne took a deep breath. 'I will not be pushed into marrying any Tom, Dick or Harry to suit you or anyone else,' she declared boldly.

'We'll see,' Agnes sneered, 'and you'll think yourself lucky if any man consents to have the likes of you.'

The seed of revolt enlarged. 'I won't!' Anne replied hotly.

Agnes' hand whipped out and cracked venomously across Anne's right cheek, making her head rock on her shoulders. Anne gasped with shock and pain, then her spirit freed itself at last. With a speed which astounded both of them, her own right hand swung and landed with an equally loud bang on Agnes' face. Although Agnes had the extra weight she also carried considerable fat. Anne was younger, and tempered by hard manual labour. Her blow was accurate, solid and completely unexpected. Agnes' head lifted high, she blinked, lost her balance and crashed down on her ample buttocks, sending a stool flying. Her skirt shot up, revealing long drawers and her cheeks were flamed with shock, anger and humiliation.

'Don't you ever dare hit me again!' cried Anne, shouting down at her. 'I'm sick of being pushed around by everyone and now it finishes. No one will ever hit me again and get away with it. I am a person, not an animal!'

'Why, you little—!'

'I'll not stop here another minute either!' Anne screeched. Her temper filled her with exultation, she felt a new person and had no idea how she had changed. Her eyes burned with wrath to match her flaming cheeks, and her thick hair swung as she tossed her head.

'What'll you do then? Be a whore like your mother?' Agnes screeched back as she scrambled to her feet, mortified, and also taken aback at the girl's unexpected fury. She itched to lash out again, but did not quite dare. Who would have thought this mouse of a girl had such a side to her? She was a harridan. Agnes took a deep breath of righteous indignation. 'You needn't think you get a

9

character from me either!' she shouted again, determined to have the last victorious word. 'I'll see you get no work anywhere and you needn't think of trying the Hiring Fair either. I'll queer your pitch there as well. You wait until the new Master hears about this. You have assaulted me. I'll set the Sheriff on you!'

Reason returned to Anne, and she half turned, stunned with herself, but not in the slightest bit sorry. Agnes' doom-laden words were frightening but, she told herself, as if I'd want to stay here anyhow. She would go to Bristol and make a new life, somewhere, somehow.

She ran from the kitchen, pell mell, back up to her attic room. Money! She must have money, and the trouble was her old master, her father, had been niggardly. All she had to show for years of labour were a few precious pennies dolled out on Boxing Day.

She slammed her door shut and halted, suddenly beset with fear of the unknown. Her fine-sounding words had a sharp, hollow ring up here. This room was all she had ever known. It was hers and hers alone. She never had to share, so the shut door represented security. She hesitated only another moment then, gritting her teeth, knelt and removed her precious pennies from their hiding place in the corner of the straw mattress. Ruefully, she surveyed her clothes. She only had one other gown, a dark brown woollen affair which

Master had given her only recently, because she had grown so. Her fingers touched it. At the time, the dress had seemed magnificent but, with feeling, she realised it was cheap and common. She had one other petticoat, a spare change of small clothes, and that was all. Grimacing a little, she bundled it all up, and fastened it with cord. From force of habit when milking there was always a length of cord around her waist used to hitch up her skirt.

Anne studied the laths and her gaze travelled to the ceiling corner, which always let in the rain, and was constantly black with mould. For years she had studied the ceiling and rough floorboards, hating them, yet impotent until now. Suddenly, these became quite precious with familiarity and alarm shot into her throat.

What had come over her? Only yesterday she had been quiet, placid and obedient, as content with her lot as any servant could be. It was eavesdropping at the Will's reading, which had upset her mental equilibrium, which had in turn been fuelled by Agnes' comments. She dithered a few more seconds, daunted by the unknown, then her new resolve hardened.

She eyed the sky through half-open shutters. There were still a number of hours before dusk, but it would be impossible to walk to Bristol before nightfall. Anne shrugged. It would not rain tonight, she could easily sleep rough, and her next thought was food. Dare she invade the kitchen to plunder the larder? Fresh pride filled her heart. She wanted nothing from this place, except to be shot of it. She clomped down the servants' stairs, past Agnes' superior room, and at the bottom Agnes awaited. There was a thundercloud on her face, and her eyes were filled with contempt.

Anne halted. With a thumping heart but as with much dignity as she could muster, she strolled past the older woman and stepped through the back door to the outside. To one side, cattle lowed, and for a few seconds she thought of her favourite, Buttercup. Who would milk them? With an impatient toss to her head, she strolled on. Now was the time to look after number one.

'Good riddance to you!' Agnes bellowed at her retreating back, then the door slammed with a final, resounding thud.

Anne lifted her head high, but her nostrils were pinched as she stepped on the dusty road which ran from Yate to Bristol. Why did she feel a prickle at the back of her eyes? How stupid, she berated herself, because, at long last, she was free. What happened now and where she ended up was a destiny held in her own hands. Abruptly, her mood lightened and fear was replaced with anticipation. Bristol! It was only a name because she had never left the village of Yate but she had listened avidly to everything old Jacob had said at the communal table. She knew in her bones there would be opportunity there, and she walked on more quickly. Her heavy black ankle boots raised a tiny dust cloud in her wake.

She soon left the intermediate village cottages behind and knew there was only the large Penford house to pass. Those of the Clothiers were in the other direction, and then the open road was hers.

Old Lady Sarah Penford watched her approach and was puzzled. She had taken a chair and installed it in her front garden, where she could bask her old limbs in the sun. Her wrinkled face was partially upturned to the yellow rays but, from an eye corner, she had spotted a figure nearing. Although her sight had deteriorated with her years, it was still fairly good and her attention was drawn to the lone figure walking so purposefully.

As she identified the girl she sat up straighter, bewildered. This girl should be working, not walking the road as if she owned it. Why did she carry that bundle under her arm and what was she doing striding in Bristol's direction? Although no beauty as the word was understood, there was something arresting about Anne Howard, which held the eye. She bristled with health and vigour. Her cheeks were a combination of sun and weather, and something else? She was tall and strong, and now carried herself with astonishing assurance. Yet this was the girl the

13

old lady had always considered a nonentity.

'Anne Howard! You girl! Come here,' she called suddenly. 'I want to talk to you!'

Anne broke stride with surprise, hesitated, then automatically obeyed. She approached the half-open front gate and stood uncertainly a few feet from the village's oldest inhabitant. Anne marvelled at Lady Sarah's age and remembered the rumours associated with her going back into the terrible times of the civil wars. Stories had it that this lady had been an active courier first for one side and then the other with a husband as daring as herself. She became aware of discerning eyes fixed on her as twin probes.

'What are you doing, and where are going at this hour?' Sarah demanded imperiously.

Anne lowered her gaze for a second, then held the sharp old eyes again. She was suddenly aware she was a minor and her rights were minimal. She doubted anyone would care though.

'I'm going into Bristol, my lady,' she replied politely.

Sarah was taken aback. 'What on earth for?'

'To make my own way in life, and not be at the beck and call of bullies any more!' Anne replied with feeling. 'No one cares now my old master is dead, and no one is telling me who to marry either!' she explained carefully, awaiting an adverse reaction.

Sarah sat back in her chair and sensed a

14

story, but doubted whether she'd get more than a watered-down version if she probed. She would satisfy this curiosity, because few gossiped harder than country people.The girl's eyes regarded her carefully, but without duplicity. If anything they were almost naïve.

'Do you have any money?'

Anne nodded. 'Some pennies!' she explained carefully, and waited.

The old lady's lips tightened. It did not take great imagination to guess how few these were. Jacob Selwell had been well-known for parsimony. She struggled from her chair. 'Wait here for me!' she ordered briskly, and slowly walked back up the path to her house.

Inside, the old lady ignored her servants, and hunted for her reticule. Anyone who walked away from both job and home was either very brave or incredibly stupid, and she had a shrewd suspicion the latter description would never apply to Anne Howard. She selected a pound coin, then paused, thinking deeply before going to her kitchen. Her housekeeper eyed her with surprise, but passed no comment. The dear old lady had always been a law unto herself and age had not diminished this one jot.

Anne fidgeted uncertainly. Time was passing, but it would be impolite to depart before the old lady returned. Then she gave a little sigh as Lady Sarah appeared, something in one hand.

'Here, girl!' Sarah said as she reached the gate. She was more tired than she realised and was irritated with the handicaps of old age. She too had once been young and bold, living through dangerous experiences, but she was too astute to feel envy. 'Take this coin. It is a gold sovereign, be very careful where you hide it and where and when you change it. Here is some bread and cheese!'

Anne's face broke into a grateful smile. 'Thank you, my lady. I didn't have any food, because I'd just had a thundering row with the housekeeper Agnes. Thank you ever so much!'

The old lady's face cracked into a knowing grin. 'Anyone would row with that woman. She is pure vinegar!'

Anne's heart swelled with gratitude and once again there was a silly little prickle at the back of her eyes. She had not expected this gesture of kindness, and suddenly wished she could sit down and tell this lovely old lady everything.

'Be careful where you sleep at nights,' the old lady continued. 'There are bad characters around, and a young girl like you, all alone, would make an easy target for the wrong types. I wish you luck, Anne Howard. May God go with you. Now I'll have to sit down and you should be on your way. Get some miles behind you before nightfall!!'

Anne recognised dismissal, so bobbing a polite courtesy, she went on, her heart lighter.

With the precious coin slipped in a piece torn from her underskirt, she hid it down her bodice and walked on briskly, mulling over the day's strange events. Then she began the hunt for somewhere to sleep as the sun dropped to the west. Who would have thought to receive such kindness from an old lady?

She concentrated upon the locality, munching the bread and cheese, eyeing everywhere. There were no hayricks here, and she was able to work out that she must be not too far distant from Mistress Margaret Penford's home and land, so there would be nothing but open countryside for miles.

She studied a copse of trees, then stepped forward and looked up. They were deciduous with a sprinkling of brambles and briers, growing in untidy heaps. The grass was thick with many dried fronds still standing from last year. Old leaves had mulched down, and she knew this was as good a place as any. Somewhere near to hand, she heard the tinkle of a stream and became aware of thirst. Carefully, straining to listen, she picked her way between the trees on an animal trail until she found the brook. It gurgled clean and sweet-tasting, then she sank back on her heels.

It was all so quiet. The birds had roosted, and the owls were not yet hunting. Far distant, over the evening air, came the sound of cattle settling down, but of man there was no hint. She stood and padded back to the brambles, laid down her bundle, unfastened it and placed her spare gown on the grasses. She lay on it and tucked the loose ends around as the coverlet. With hands under her head, she stared up at the stars and felt blissfully at peace with the world, and quite unconcerned at what the morning might bring. She was completely and totally free.

Very gradually she sank into sleep, half-curled in a ball, the light sleep in which the senses are not at total rest. She woke abruptly and lay frozen, wits startled into action, unable to understand where she was for a few seconds.

The stars were clear in one area of the sky but played hide and seek with clouds from the east. There was a slight breeze, softly touching one cheek as she sat upwards before slowly and quietly sitting. Instinct made her movements silent, though her thumping heart sounded as a drum in her ears.

Ripples went down her spine in small, cold waves, and she shivered involuntarily as her senses jabbed a warning. With a dry throat she stood uneasily, thankful for the cover from the trees. She strained her ears. What had awoken her? It was very dark to one side, with faint visibility on the other, then the moment vanished, and she could see very little at all.

Very gradually sounds reached her and she held her breath with shock. Voices! At the same time, the wind fluffed from another angle and a familiar scent caused her to stiffen with fresh shock. Somewhere near to hand was a horse that had been ridden hard, fast, and sweated.

Perspiration dappled her forehead, and she did not know what to do. Half of her wanted to stay discreetly hidden, but her other more natural instinct demanded a curious investigation.

Anne was baffled why anyone should be in this remote spot at this time but there was no doubt, somewhere very close to hand, was a horse. No farm workers owned such valuable animals, which indicated the animal's owner must be gentry but why was he here? Very gradually, she was able to pick out the muted rumble of voices and her eyes opened wider . . . Two people?

She hesitated only a few more seconds, then curiosity overcame caution. Biting her bottom lip, straining to be careful, she padded forward, careful to avoid the dead twigs or noisy, dried leaves. She dodged low branches, and, with dry lips and bated breath, tiptoed forward.

A sharp sound on her right made her freeze. There was a chink of metal as a horse ground on its bit, then a soft snort. She stood on her toes, peeped between a shrub's topmost twigs at the identical moment that the moon obliged. It silvered down, and she caught her breath with astonishment. There were two horses as well as a pony.

A man stood with his back towards her, bent forward, talking in a low tone to a much smaller figure. Anne could see he was exceedingly tall and wore a modern coat with sleeves, fine breeches, and shoes with ornate buckles. There was a sword on his left and when he moved slightly, his coat parted, and she made out the ugly, dark colour of a pistol.

The man half-turned and Anne studied a handsome face with a high forehead, fine cheekbones and balanced lips. His hair was a thick, dark brown with the suggestion of natural curls. As her eyes adjusted to the gloom, she studied the other much smaller figure who was partially obscured by the first man, then the moon vanished again.

A small sack was handed from the man to his companion. Then he spoke again. 'Go now!' he said in a cultured voice. 'Get home safely. I'll be in touch when I can!'

The smaller person muttered something indistinguishable before turning to the pony. He scrambled up in an ungainly fashion, and the tall man passed up a sack, gave a slap to the pony's quarters and the animal trotted away sharply, making the rider jolt. A bad rider, Anne told herself with amazement—one who would come off if the pony tripped over an acorn.

The tall man watched only a few seconds, then swung around briskly on his heels. He looked carefully at the two horses then, almost casually, unlimbered his pistol.

'You can come out now,' he growled. 'I'll count to five, then shoot!'

TWO

Anne's heart lurched as she realised it was the horses that had given her away; both heads stared in her direction, ears pricked, nostrils expanded as they took in her scent. How foolish she had been. Now the man looked directly towards her, pistol held steady, though surely he could not see her? Did he bluff?

She saw his finger start to tighten and Anne whipped around, nearly stumbled, regained her balance and bolted. Any second she expected to hear the pistol's bark as it sent a ball into the back. The man was taken by surprise and bellowed with anger.

She fled for her life yet still managed to think straight. She dare not run in the open when up against horses but how deep did this covert go? She veered sharply aside, ducked under a whippy sapling's lower branch, pushing through a small shrub, then flung herself behind the protection of a very old oak.

He blundered after her, but now the moon became an ally. Another large trough of clouds scurried as the wind strengthened and

21

illumination varnished. She heard the man halt abruptly, curse, and guessed he was listening for her. She calculated roughly where he must be as her mind raced. She was under no illusions now. If she wished to live, she had to reduce the odds.

The man hesitated, then moved off at a tangent, his steps positive rather than slow, so, making up her mind, she warily backtracked, taking infinite pains to be quiet. With pauses to try and estimate his direction, she headed back to the horses whose reins, she had noticed, were only held with a slipknot. Once she heard a twig crack on one side and nerves made a giggle arise again. How long would it take him to get her ploy?

She hurried the final few steps, then slowed automatically, as she had been taught. She let the horses take in her scent, as she whispered sweet nothings to them, while unfastening the reins. Every nerve screamed at her to rush, but she knew better. The horses sniffed, then stood quietly; she slid into the saddle of one, praying the girth was secure, for there was no time to check. It was still tight, and it hit her—this man's rendezvous was pre-planned and of a natural, short duration.

Her mount fidgeted once at her light weight, then stilled. She touched with her heels and moved in the opposite direction, leading the spare horse. A snap look around showed the man was nowhere in sight, and she heeled again, making her mount jiggle eagerly. The lead horse yawed awkwardly in the uncooperative way of all horses but, gritting her teeth, she forced herself to be patient.

Then her mount broke into a short, snappy canter and the other horse copied, anxious not to be left behind as the herd instinct took over. Anne neck-reined sideways to head for the open countryside. Only a few more paces, and the path was free from trees and grasses and stretched ahead in a rippling sward, dappled by the moon.

She was going to succeed! Suddenly there was a bellow to her rear, and she heeled sharply, conscious of the pistol he carried. She must gallop for safety. Then a shrill whistle knifed the air. It was very high pitched, at the top grade of human hearing and Anne's mount recognised it, obeying instantly. The horse halted abruptly, dropped his head and bucked hard, with a back arched and tail clamped against stiff quarters while hooves drummed on firm ground.

The other horse shied sideways in panic, the reins jerked from Anne's grasp as she rocked savagely, taken completely unawares. She grabbed the pommel as the horse bucked again, ears flat to his head, which sank lower, between straight forelegs.

Anne shuddered. Her body jolted, then whiplashed, and she knew she was beaten. Her spine cracked with pain as her balance left.

Her body flew from the saddle and hurtled down to earth harshly. She rolled over twice and ended up with a dull thud against the man's legs.

She lay winded and badly scared, her senses bemused before she slowly scrambled to her feet. The man swiftly replaced his pistol and grabbed her arm. She fought frantically, terror giving additional strength, reflexes quick. She kicked out, spitting like a cat and aimed for his groin.

The man brought his right hand around and cracked her left cheek. For the second time she went flying, and lay prone, winded, uncertain.Then a long-dormant temper exploded for the second time in twenty-four hours.

She jumped up and sprang forward. The man was shocked, he'd suspected she would be more likely try to retreat. Anne hit out with her own exceedingly powerful right hand. Her blow was devastatingly accurate and out of the blue. It smashed on the man's cheek with enough force to make him stagger backwards and blink with the shock of her temper. It had not dawned upon him to expect resistance from a young female.

His lips tightened with annoyance, as his handsome face changed to a cold mask. Quickly he withdrew his sword.

'One more movement and I'll skewer you!' he rasped.

Anne spat at him, spittle hitting his right cheek. She was outraged, trembling with temper, all fear evaporated.

'Why you little hellcat, you!' he snarled at her, wiping his face with his free hand.

Anne, opened her mouth to roar back, then snapped it shut. How to get away from him without injury? The horses stood uneasily, reins dangling with one set half-hooked on a bush.

'What the hell are you doing here at this time of night? What did you see and hear!' he roared at her. 'Answer me!'

'I—I—nothing!' Anne shot back, chest heaving with wrath, as she watched the sword's tip.

'You little liar!' he bellowed back. 'Why are you here?'

Anne regained her wits. 'Why are *you* here?' she retorted, and felt fear mingle with rage. There was a nasty look in his eyes. How could she have thought him handsome? His expression was bleak and cruel, his eyes two hard dots, which bored through her. She noted wide shoulders, which meant great strength. Neither had she missed his speed and grace, and from him there came an aura of calculated ferocity. Suddenly she gulped uncertainly, nearly terrified, but struggling not to show this.

Of the two, he was the more shocked. Richard Mason was a product of the times. He was capable of changing from smooth politeness to total ruthlessness in a second, because he had learned long ago that life was precarious—only a fool let drop his guard yet this girl had crept up on him!

He examined her more carefully, as the clouds finally slid away. In the full moon he took in every detail and his expert eyes immediately categorised her status. She was a servant, but a healthy, strong one judging by the blow she had slammed on his face. Was it coincidence, she was here, though? Chance was always haphazard and rare, but it did happen. A tiny idea shot into his mind, still nebulous, and he pursed his lips. He could not think about it now.

'It's my place to question you,' he rasped coldly. 'For the last time, what were you doing here?'

Anne hesitated, aware now how pitifully thin her story would sound to a stranger. How to placate him enough to make him drop his guard?

'I'm on my way into Bristol, if you must know,' she snapped back. 'I'm walking and it is a long way.'

'From where?' he barked.

Anne nodded to her rear. 'The village back there. I had a row and I've left my place. And I'm not wanted anyhow now my master is dead, and I'll not work for the new one,' she told him, then shrugged. 'What's it to you?'

'I'll ask again what you overheard,' he

growled coldly.

Ann flashed resentment. 'I've told you. Nothing! Do you have cloth ears?'

'Don't get smart with me, brat!'

'You don't scare me, Mr Man! You stand there, all high, mighty and pompous. Just because you have a sword and a pistol against a helpless, little defenceless female!' she mocked and held her breath. Would he rise to her taunting bait?

He snorted. 'Helpless, my foot. When you can land a blow like a horse's kick! And I think you're a spoiled miss, who needs a thoroughly good hiding.'

'And I suppose you think you're the one to try?'

Anne marvelled at herself. It was crazy the way the pair of them stood here, in the middle of the night, trading insults. She felt a crazy wave of hysteria rise, but fought it away. She could only provoke him so far, but get away from him she must.

'I'm coming round to that idea,' he drawled at her with exasperation. He thought back. It was true, he had stood with his back to her, hiding his companion so identification had obviously been impossible. For the second time, the idea entered his head, and it had grown a little. She would have to come with him, and thank God that at least she could ride and astride like a man. Wasn't that a strange accomplishment for a serving wench? He

27

scented some peculiar story, then made up his mind.

'You are coming with me,' he growled. 'Get on that bay horse, and don't try any tricks. This will be right behind you,' he said, giving the tiniest prick, with his sword.

Anne gulped. She had no intention of going anywhere with him because everything about him now seemed highly dangerous. She racked her brains, but no sensible plan appeared. She eyed him. His face was an implacable mask. All the natural female ploys shot through her mind to be rejected forthwith. This big man was too sure of himself, and a little too worldly wise to fall for female foibles.

She moved a step and halted. 'My bundle!' she gasped. 'That's all I have in the world!'

'Get it and look sharp about it!'

Anne ran back to her sleeping place and, while he stood guard, she packed her flimsy possessions, then tied then with one of the many pieces of cord around her waist.

'Move!' he barked at her, and his sword gave a little nip at one shoulder blade.

Anne flinched, scowled, but did as she was told. What an odd, noxious man he was, yet what could she yet do? He watched her as she approached the horse, and this time Anne was careful. She checked the girth, shortened the stirrups and swung into the saddle with practised ease.

He was baffled as he copied. Something did

not ring quite true. For a serving wench she moved around horses as an expert and his ever-suspicious mind revolved once more.

'You ride ahead. You put one toenail wrong and you will get a ball in your back. And I do not bluff, either!' he announced coldly.

'No, I bet you don't!' Anne told herself wildly, while her heart thundered again. Who was he? What was he doing here? What did he intend to do with her? She bit her lip, as fear flooded her heart. It was all very well, showing the defiance but what now?

Richard Mason eyed her stiff back, and then gave a tiny shake to his head. Was it really possible such a gutsy girl could be useful? But how to tame her? Was he going mad? He gave a tiny push to his back muscles, aware he was getting short of sleep. He had intended to cold camp on this night, after his meeting but now there was nothing for it but to get out of this area as fast as possible. A missing girl would certainly arouse a hue and cry; the last thing he wanted. He knew if he had any sense, he would kill the girl here and now and be done with it. As it was he was saddled with a packet of trouble because he was not, for one instant, fooled by her apparent obedience. One thing was certain though, he must find out about her. The equestrian expertise she displayed was that only equalled by a handful of gentry females. If only time had been available to make investigations but time was never on his

29

side nowadays.

Anne rode with a thumping heart and dry throat. She felt a sudden nausea arise and, swallowing hard, only just managed to stop herself from vomiting. She forced her stomach into calmness, gave a little shake to her head and made herself think again.

'Ride west!' he grunted from behind her. 'Not that way, turn left, girl!'

His tone aroused another wave of fury, but she stifled back a retort. She must concentrate. What was his game? Where did he plan to take her, and, more to the point, why? She thought about him. Both his speech and clothing gave away his superior class, far higher than that of old Jacob. Yet he also had this dangerous aura, coupled with arrogance and self-confidence, which she had never met before. Escape was going to be exceedingly difficult, but at least she was mounted and stay in the saddle she would this time. Surely both horses could not have been trained to a whistle? This was highly unlikely. His was a better animal. Its flashy limbs showed breeding, speed and stamina. Yet he was of a nondescript colour. A horse that could mingle with hundreds of others. Her own mount was better than any Jacob had offered, which also indicated breeding. For a second or two, she thought back wistfully to only last week, before Jacob had been thrown and broken his neck. What would he have thought about all this? Would he have cared enough to search for her? When it came down to it, who did care? She was quite alone, any escape must arise from her own brain. She objected to this abduction. She fumed at his treatment and her new spirit boiled with barely controlled anger. Think she told herself! Think of all ways to escape from him!

'Now turn east!' he ordered. 'The other way, of course. Don't you know the area?' he asked sarcastically.

Of course, she didn't, Anne told herself silently, she had never been given a chance to learn it.

He eyed her dubiously. She was riding just too quietly, for his peace of mind. Of what was she thinking? One thing was for certain they could hardly ride for hours like a pair of mutes.

'What's your name?' he asked, pushing his horse alongside hers, though keeping the sword prudently in his right hand.

Anneiqu threw him a cold look. He was obviously offering some kind of belated olive branch. 'Mind your own business!' she told him acidly.

'Grow up!' he threw back at her.

Anne reined back, turned and glowered at him, a wary eye on his sword. She itched to question him. then a thought entered her head. He was simply a male, albeit bigger and stronger than her but men, she had learned long ago from old Jacob, could have an insatiable curiosity, far worse than women's. Was it possible she could have a weapon against him with her silence? Better something than nothing for the time being. She averted her eyes, stared ahead and pushed her mount forward once more.

'Oh! We have a fit of the sulks now, do we?' he mocked, both amused and annoyed. He must find out about her. Information was always imperative to him. He had expected his question to arouse a tirade of feminine hysteria, so her silence piqued and intrigued. This one definitely did not come from the common mould.

'My name is Richard Mason,' he offered quietly and waited. 'I'd like to know yours?'

Anne continued to ignore him as they rode under the moon. She studiously stared between her horse's ears and examined what she could see of the landscape. Surely that was dawn coming over there with the slightest flush of pink? There was not a soul around. The land was empty, she realised, and, for a few seconds, her spirit quailed.

'A one-sided conversation gets boring,' he continued in a milder tone.

Anne ignored him and continued to think carefully. A little idea had shot into line. She turned it over carefully, almost flinching at its flimsiness. Rack her brains as she might though, she could think of nothing else. Around her waist was still a long length of cord, and with one hand she slowly unfastened this. On his blind side she started to make a series of knots, one on top of the other gradually building up a tiny hardball. It took time, in which they covered a few more miles and dawn came up properly, removing the shadows so trees stood proud and aloof in odd patches.

Keeping an impassive face, she felt the cord end which now ended in a small, hardball of numerous, simple knots. It seemed a feeble weapon but was the best she could come up with. Gradually, she let herself slump in the saddle, the picture of exhaustion with bowed head.

He frowned and rode a little nearer, wondering just how fatigued she really was. He had no idea what she might have undergone the hours before they met, and there were many more miles they must ride before another night.

'Are you all right?' he asked quickly. A sick or fainting girl would be the end.

Anne took a wild chance. Now was as good a time as any. She drew back her right hand, while at the same time she used the reins and dug with just one heel. Her horse was shocked but obeyed as the high part of his curb bit bruised a sensitive mouth. The horse turned on its hocks and cannoned into his mount. At the same time, Anne whirled her crude weapon in the man's face. He was taken

33

completely by surprise.

More by good luck than judgment the hard, little knot landed square across his face, cutting deeply, a slightly frayed end whipping into one eye. For a second he was blinded. Anne swung again, as his horse shied and this time the hard knot landed on bunched quarters. The man's horse objected and kicked wildly. He had no chance at all. Half blinded, stung with the unexpected pain he swayed in the saddle, lost his balance and went flying in a graceful parabola.

Anne rammed with her heels and released the reins. Her horse shot forward in a frantic gallop, and she screeched at him. She stood in the stirrups, weight neatly balanced over sliding shoulders, hands low beside a whipping black mane.

'Faster!' she screamed, and her horse, ears flattened, responded, startled by this virago on his back. His hooves hammered the ground while at the same time Anne gazed sharply from right to left, desperate to see signs of habitation and a rescue. Surely there had to be a village nearby, and not far away, because right ahead, the grassland changed to ridge and furrow.

It was full day now and the earth was damp with dew. It glistened in the cobwebs as they hurtled along and she knew what happened instantly. Her horse's off fore leg landed on a furrow and slipped. The animal strained to recover its balance, pecked badly, then slowly, remorselessly, it fell. Again she left the saddle and landed with a thump, rolling inelegantly in an untidy muddy heap, while her horse galloped off gleefully kicking to both sides.

Anne turned her head. Where was he? Already coming up fast was a bobbing blur. And she remembered the whistle-trained horse. She whipped her head to stare in the other direction. Was that the plume of early-morning smoke?

She was badly winded and could only lie there, tears flooding her eyes as he thundered up. So near but so far away. Was this where he would kill her? If only she had waited until full light showed a more suitable terrain.

He rode up and sat still a moment, glowering down at her. Water cascaded from one eye, while Anne looked up at him, face and clothing filthy from red mud. She struggled to maintain an impassive face though real terror almost choked her as he dismounted and methodically placed sword and pistol to one side. His well-trained horse stood still, just stretching his neck a little.

He stepped nearer and their eyes locked. Richard Mason seethed with rare, hot anger. This girl had provoked him beyond measure, and now she still had the effrontery to glower up at him instead of cringing. He breathed hard, as his eyes ranged over her.

The fall had ripped an already threadbare

gown. On one side, the bodice had split from shoulder to waist. Lying half on her side, her breasts showed as enticing invitations. Her skirt was halfway up her thighs and her legs sprawled inelegantly, covered with wet mud. Her drawers had slipped halfway down, and he studied plump, taut buttocks.

'You hellcat!' he said in a cold, low voice. 'There's one way to tame you!'

Anne did not miss the change in his eyes, which narrowed to slits, but also burned with a fresh emotion. In an awesome flash, she understood his intent. Panic filled her as she struggled to sit erect, and cover her limbs.

He dropped to one knee, fumbled with the drawstring of his breeches, and roughly shoved her on her back. Anne flew into a raw panic. She pushed with her ankles to find a purchase. Then he was everywhere, his strength astounding. She hit him. She snapped with her teeth. She tried to knee his groin, then he had spread-eagled her legs, hovered and drove into her flesh.

A shriek rose in her throat as raw pain consumed her. His hard penis crashed through her dry flesh, then, for a second, their eyes met. Hers were pinpoint dots of pain while his registered confusion. Then his sex drive mounted and Anne felt his waves grow faster almost smothering her as he drove to his climax.

Finally red-faced, panting hard, he halted,

head bowed, and Anne felt the tears streaming down her cheeks. He pulled away from her and she made an ineffectual attempt to claw his eyes. Then as he stood, she turned on her flank and sobbed. It had all been too much.

Richard Mason was stunned, completely taken aback. Her genuine distress sent guilt into his heart. 'I'm sorry' he said in a low voice. 'I never thought, I mean, what I'm trying to say is!'

Anne lifted a miserable face. 'You think just because I'm a servant. I'm available for any man. I was a virgin!' she wailed.

'Oh God!' he groaned, coming to his senses at last.

Anne closed her eyes and willed the tears to stop. She turned to look up at him. 'You thought I was any old bitch on heat!' she accused.

Her words struck home, and he flinched. It was the first time in his life he had taken sex by brute force. He bent, and, biting his lip, gently touched one dirty arm.

'I mean it when I'm saying I'm sorry, but you drive a man insane!'

'So that gives you rights, does it?' Anne screeched at him. 'I hate you. What if you have made me pregnant?'

He flinched again at this, and his eyes opened wide to flare their whites. This was something he had not considered.

'Rapist!' she hurled at him. 'I'll kill you for

what you've done to me if I become pregnant!'

'Oh Christ!' he blasphemed. 'I know mere words can't change what's happened but I swear by God I never dreamed you were still a virgin. Can we start again. Please?' he begged placating. He was disgusted with his lack of self-discipline and he could imagine what would be said to him from another quarter.

THREE

Anne struggled to stand, dragging the tattered gown around her in a pathetic attempt at decency, but failed completely. He turned, walked back to his saddlebag and returned, hand outstretched.

'What's that?' Anne asked miserably.

'Cold meat and bread. I've a small skin of wine too. I know this is not the most ideal place but shall we try and start again?'

Anne's stomach growled. She was used to good, plain food served regularly and it was hours since she had wolfed down Lady Sarah's offering. Her mouth watered.

He carefully divided the food, then gave her the larger share. She took it without hesitation, snatched a bite, then remembered her manners and started to eat more daintily. For a fewer crazy seconds her humour almost took over. Here they were, standing in a muddy ploughed field, eating after she had been raped. Was she going mad, or was it the world in general?

Richard eyed her carefully. Her temper had subsided yet the tears had left clean runnels down her dirty cheeks. They ate in silence, each lost in complicated thought. He finished first, wiped his hands on the seat of his breeches, and took a deep breath:

'You may be right,' he admitted heavily, 'in which case the responsibility is mine and mine alone. If I have made you pregnant, I will look after you. That I vow. I was going to ditch you a few miles away while I rode off. I would not have harmed a female,' he emphasised, and now knew he meant it despite his rigid training. 'But, because of what I have done I think you should come back to my house in London.'

Anne blinked with shock. 'London?' she parroted. If his home was in London, what on earth had he been doing in this part of her shire, which was over a hundred miles from the capital? And who had been the mysterious third person? What had they been up to? London! The capital was at the other end of the world. All she had been able to think about was Bristol. Her curiosity was vitally alive. London—and she rolled the name around. Wasn't that where everything happened? Never in her wildest thoughts had she envisaged a trip to the capital, and suddenly

39

her blood stirred. She swallowed the last of the food, licked her lips, wished there was more, then wiped her hands on her backside as he had done.

'Doing what?' she asked warily.

'Be a companion to me and perhaps even a friend,' he asked her in a gentle tone, tongue in cheek. He could already imagine the caustic comments about to be thrown at him from that quarter. 'I know it sounds mad, but I live in a fairly big house, with only servants. No one to talk to of an evening. It would be nice to come home and find a friend,' and he paused delicately.

Anne narrowed her eyes. Friend? Did he think she was that naive and had grown up under a gooseberry bush? What was his real motive? There was nothing to stop him riding off right now. So why didn't he? Something smelled grossly false yet she knew she was intrigued. London—her heart throbbed. Once there, the whole world might be within her grasp. This mystery man—who would be made to pay—was someone she could use to her advantage. She struggled to keep her features impassive while her mind raced. She certainly had nothing to lose and she admitted the mystery around him was tantalising to her natural curiosity, yet she refused to acquiesce immediately.

'I don't think we would have much to discuss because you are the gentry and I'm only a servant!' she said bluntly.

He shook his head. 'I asked for that,' he agreed, striving to be pleasant, but conscious time was passing, and there was a long way to ride. 'Think about it,' he suggested quietly. 'We'll find somewhere to spend the night, while you make up your mind. I won't bother you again, unless you want me to,' he added, meaning it.

'Liar!' Anne thought. Unknown to him, she was extremely well versed because old Jacob had travelled to London now and again to visit his nephew. Upon his return he had always regaled his workers at the dining table, and no one had been a more avid listener than her.

'Are you one of these rich men?' she asked suddenly, with no tact at all.

He was surprised at this.' I'm not rolling in money,' he replied after a pause, 'but I'm not short either.'

Anne frowned, puzzled. 'What do you do then, is your money inherited?' she persisted. 'I should know something about you,' she ended a little feebly, as his eyes narrowed with annoyance. 'I am not just being nosy!'

Richard made a snap decision. This girl came from such a rare and unusual mould that instinct told him it would be prudent to give some of the truth as bait.

'I'm a highwayman!'

Anne was flabbergasted. If he had said, he travelled to the moon daily she could not have been that taken aback.

'I am a member of a particular organisation. Wild's!'

Anne remained speechless, struggling to assimilate this gem of information. 'You steal?'

His mood changed at her bewilderment and the awe in her voice. He grinned, his face becoming more friendly, almost boyish. He nodded at her horse.

Anne stared at the animal, who had wandered back to join a companion. 'Him?' she asked with stunned amazement.

'And anything else worth having!' he told her quietly, very amused at the complex thoughts which flitted across her face. Somewhere, he sensed Mother Church had had a hand in her morals but how strong were they when put to the real test?

'What organisation and who is Mr Wild?' she asked, struggling to come to terms with this information.

He took a very deep breath. 'What I have just told you is more than enough to get me murdered!' he remarked very seriously.

'What!'

He nodded solemnly. 'I am not being melodramatic, either. If you would like to come with me, I can explain as we ride,' he offered, adding extra bait to his hook.

Anne never hesitated as her mind worked with rapidity. She would go with him, she would hear what he had to say, she certainly would experience life in the rich man's home in London. There would be ample time to plot a revenge for what he had done but what if she were pregnant? This latter thought made her gulp, then her mind switched in another direction. She nodded at the horse that had returned.

'Someone could recognise him!'

He gave a rich chuckle, and the transformation astounded her. He changed into a mischievous boy and it flashed through her mind that this Richard Mason was a far more complex character than she had initially realised.

'Not where he'll be sold!' he told her, and laughed at the thunderstruck look on her face. Then he became serious again, and changed back to the stern man. 'There will be a lot I cannot and will not tell you,' he began firmly, 'but I don't think you'll be bored in London after life in a village. What do you say? Friends?' And he offered his hand.

Anne hesitated only fractionally, then grasped it. She had nothing to lose, and perhaps more to gain than she had ever envisaged before.

'What work will I be expected to do?' she asked, hesitantly.

He frowned a second, his turn to be taken aback. Then he understood, and softened a little. 'My guests do not work!' he told her quickly. 'I have my own servants, who run my house, and I know better than to interfere with them. You could do much as you like, especially when I'm away, which happens often. I have a young serving girl who can wait on you. Indeed, young Kate might even make a friend. I don't suppose you can read or write?'

Anne bridled. 'I can read, write and figure rather well,' she replied hotly.

His eyebrows rose. This was stranger and stranger. Whoever heard of a servant with education, and who could ride as well as she did? There was much it would be prudent to learn about her.

'Would I have to bed you because I lived in your house?' she asked, suddenly wanting to know where she stood, feeling resentment rear its head again.

He took a deep breath. 'Not unless it was your choice,' he replied firmly, flinching a little at the sudden hardness in her eyes. This girl was far more complicated than he had imagined possible. Who exactly was she? He had a flaring presentiment she was deep and would only ever tell him what she wanted him to know but time pressed urgently now.

'Let's ride then!' he said, and eyed her clothing. 'I'll get you something new to wear. When we find an inn for the night. Bear with me until later. I've a spare cloak behind my saddle. Cover yourself with that.'

Anne was grateful and took the proffered

cloak. At least it hid her breasts, and she felt a sudden yearning to wash and cleanse herself.

They rode in silence for a while, because Richard felt uncertain how to start a conversation while Anne was consumed with a ridiculous shyness. He realised it was up to him as they cantered on, knee to knee.

'You looked so wild, untamed and beautiful back there—' he started. Then stilled uncertainly, as she flashed him a sardonic look.

'Beautiful?' Anne snorted. 'I learned long ago that's one thing I am not, and neither do I like blatant flattery'

'It's not flattery!' he protested swiftly, taken aback at her bitter tone. For God's sake, from what kind of place had she come? His words had been said with sincerity, and he hastened to stress this, suddenly anxious to show his better side. 'I mean, what I say. I agree you are no court beauty. But what man really wants painted cheeks and flowered hair? I don't, that's for sure. Your beauty is unique to you, because it is wild and ethereal.'

Anne turned this over in her mind, her suspicions subsiding, a little. She liked that description. He watched her carefully, anxious to keep her pliant and peaceful. 'Tell me about yourself,' he invited in a soft tone.

She did in a few brief words. 'It simply never entered my head that my master was my real father. I suppose I was naïve,' she ended thoughtfully, 'not that knowing would have done me any good.'

'I still don't know your name!'

She turned to him. Now he wore his handsome face. 'It's Anne Howard.'

He swiftly lifted an imaginary hat from his head, and, with a sweep of his right arm, performed a courtly bow in the saddle.

Anne giggled, gloriously bursting into laughter. He looked so funny, and his eyes twinkled like a little boy's again. He was entertaining, but she reflected going quietly serious, which was the true man? This jovial gallant or the cold-faced killer?

Richard wondered at what she now thought. Her features had stilled as if she had met a new problem. 'You do have beauty,' he repeated, anxious to see the bright glow in her eyes. 'Your hair is a gorgeous rich colour, and when your eyes sparkle they are like diamonds. Don't let anyone tell you otherwise, but come on, time is flying, and we have miles to ride to a decent inn.'

They increased their speed, riding shoulder to shoulder. Anne revelled in the rush of air upon her face, but was also ruefully aware that she was unused to long hours in the saddle. Already she could feel the pull and play on muscles used only spasmodically. She had an idea the next day might find her crippled with aches and pains.

As they breasted a hill, to allow the animals to take a breather he threw a look at her. 'We will walk a couple of miles before we canter again. I always like to know my horse has plenty left in him,' he told her with a wolfish grin.

She had a smile as she took his meaning, then she frowned. 'Tell me about Wild's organisation.'

He hesitated, now regretting his earlier words. How loose-tongued would she be? Then he recalled earlier moments. When the mood took her, this girl took refuge behind an irritating silence. So hopefully she never gossiped.

'Not today. That's for tomorrow. When we are at the inn, in public, keep your mouth shut tightly and leave all the talking to me. That's for our mutual safety,' he added heavily.

Anne merely nodded. Great waves of fatigue had started to thump at her back and legs. She was short of sleep, and so was he. She marvelled at his strength and endurance. He rode easily like a fresh man. She was glad to see a small village appear, though where exactly they were she neither knew nor cared. They rode into a cobbled yard and halted thankfully, letting the horses stretch their necks.

Anne dismounted, but only with a mighty effort and would have stumbled if he had not steadied her arm. 'Courage!' he whispered in her ear. 'You have done exceedingly well.'

'I feel so dirty. Do you think I could wash?'

47

Anne asked him hopefully.

'I'll do even better than that.' Then he paused and eyed her. 'While we are here, you will be accepted as my woman with no questions being asked. You will be quite safe, but talk to no one. We'll probably have to share the same chamber, but don't worry about me,' he added hastily, as she stiffened a little.

She took a deep breath. She could not last remember when she had felt so exhausted. It took a major effort of will to walk over the yard's cobbles after the horses had been led away by the ostlers. She was appalled at the variety of pains that stabbed her muscles.

Although late afternoon there were many people around, and she still had to take it all in, while Richard held a conversation and made some arrangements. She heard the chink of coins change hands, but the innkeeper studiously ignored her. Did this mean Richard came here often with women? Suddenly, she could not care less—if she did not sit down soon, she would fall down flat on her face.

Richard came back, took her arm and guided her. He opened a side door, with familiarity, walked along a stone-flagged very long passage, which had doors off on both sides. Their room was at the extreme end, the door already open. Inside a fire burned merrily, while logs spat angry sparks and a little maid bustled around pouring pewter cans of hot water into a hip bath.

Anne eyed this hopefully, and he caught the look. 'It's for you!' he whispered. 'I'm going elsewhere to wash, after I've checked the horses, although they are pretty reliable here. The maid will assist you with your toilet and bring you fresh clothes. When she's gone though, bolt the door and open to no one but me.

She nodded firmly. All this made sense, because by his own admission he was a wanted man. As soon as he had vanished she stripped off her filthy, tattered clothing. She stepped into the hip bath gingerly, as it was a novel experience. Always before, she'd had to make do with a jug and water except in the hot weather when she had bathed in a discreet part of the local river. She inhaled. The maid had sprinkled in some delightful herbs.

' Shall I do your back, muni?'

Anne gave her a look of amazement and felt another insane giggle rise. It was the first time, she had been addressed so respectably, and it felt good. Much better than 'You get here you slut of a girl!' followed by a couple of blows.

She splashed and wallowed, oblivious to the soaking rushes, while the maid scrubbed her, then washed her hair before finally rinsing her down with extra jugs of water. She stepped out on a straw mat, and the maid wrapped her in a large robe already warmed before the bustling fire.

49

Her spirits soared despite exhaustion. Perhaps this whole adventure was going to be more fun than she had anticipated. She sank in the chair and watched the maid empty the bath into numerous jugs, trotting out somewhere to do this, then suddenly she was alone. Warm, clean, ravenously hungry. She hastily stood and slid the door bolts, then noticed clean clothing was laid out neatly on a side chair. There was a russet-coloured gown, fresh white small clothes, a crisp white underskirt and a nightgown the same. She slipped into the latter, then brushed her hair, marvelling at such luxury. Then the brisk, double rap on the door made her jump.

'Who is it?' she asked cautiously.

'It's me, Richard.'

She drew back the bolt, and he stepped in. He bristled cleanliness and wore a fresh green shirt, dark green breeches and plain black shoes without any kind of ornamentation. His whole dress was utilitarian and businesslike.

They studied each other, eyebrows lifting with mutual approval. Richard reached out one hand, and softly touched her hair, still damp in places. 'You think you lack beauty? It's a pity you can't see yourself right now,' he murmured with admiration.

Anne felt herself blush uneasily, embarrassed without quite knowing why. She sank back in a chair and studied him as he stood by the fire, feet apart, legs braced, smelling of piquant herbs. He held himself with proud dignity yet from him came a presence. It was like that of a wild, proud cat. Feral, completely untamed, with power only slightly masked.

For a few crazy seconds, she felt a wild need to lay her head on his broad chest, and she flushed again. What was the matter with her? He had raped her and for that there had to be a reckoning. Was it her wits? Her mind swirled with confusion, as she looked at her hands. They had never been so clean before. Her nails were broken and calluses stood out sharply in wide relief as a result of being immersed in the hot water.

Another rap on the door and he stilled, one hand hovering near his pistol, changing in a flash to pent-up wariness again. It was the same maid but this time she struggled in with an overloaded tray. There was a huge bowl of soup, on top of which floated plump, savoury dumplings. There were platters with beef, still a delicate red in the centre. Large chunks of bread, some fruit and two pitchers of ale.

'We will serve ourselves,' Richard said briefly, saw the maid out and bolted the door again. He fastened shutters against the night, secured them, and laid his weapons aside, but still neatly to hand, Anne noticed.

'Sit before the fire and I'll do the honours,' he told her, though briskly and quickly he gave her a bowl of soup followed by a generously

51

heaped platter.

There was silence, as they ate ravenously, their need almost frantic but they slowed for the fruit and ale. Anne sighed happily. She had never felt so good in her life. The fire's heat was welcome because the night air had chilled, and he tossed some more logs on. She was aware he had watched her covertly but she knew her eating manners were impeccable. Any who had eaten at Jacob's table had quickly acquired manners, because he had been fastidious in this respect.

She felt sleep hover. From outside still came sounds of hooves and late travellers arriving, voices were raised, orders shouted and greetings given.

'You look exhausted,' he said softly. 'You take the bed, while I'll sleep on the floor. The privy is out the back and leaves much to be desired but there is a chamber pot. I'll put these platters outside for the maid,' and he took his time, giving her a little necessary privacy.

Anne snuggled down in the bed and wrapped herself on the comforter while she regarded him with bleary eyes. He prowled a circuit of the room, once again checking its security, then he slipped off his breeches and lay down before the fire, sword and pistol to hand.

Anne felt sleep hover. She wanted to rethink all that which had happened in the past twenty-four hours, but it was all too much of an effort. The last thing she heard was a harsh grating of iron wheels on the cobbles as a late coach arrived.

The next thing she knew was a light touch on her shoulders. She awoke with a start, still bewildered and he was looking down at her and holding out a small bowl of steaming liquid.

'Yes, it is tea and just after dawn.'

'Tea!' she marvelled. Even Jacob had rarely drunk this, because of the prohibitive cost.

He grinned with amusement at her surprise, rather pleased with himself. 'I still have connections. Now I'm going to see the horses. Get dressed, when you can, and we will breakfast. The morning maid will keep an eye on the door, while I am away.

Anne nodded, stretched, then winced with agony. Her whole body was an exquisite mass of pain. She could not get on a horse today. It was quite out of the question.

FOUR

'I can't!' Anne cried out, eyeing the stirrup iron.

'You can!' he encouraged. 'You must!'

Anne gasped, as she stretched a leg tentatively upwards and looked at him wildly, shaking her head. She had never imagined her whole body could be such a mass of pain from overtaxed muscles. Even if she could manage to get on the saddle, surely she would fall off straight away?

'Use the mounting block,' he advised anxiously, understanding the state of her muscles, guiding her firmly. 'Then we will ride out and walk. You will gradually loosen. I promise.'

She wanted to believe him, but could not. When she did flop into the saddle it was as gracelessly as the movement of an empty sack. It was agony to try to grip, let alone sit up straight, but, biting her lip, she tried. He nodded his approval, as he led the way at a gentle walk.

Their horses had been corn-fed and were very fresh. 'We will have to canter to settle them down. Just ride by balance alone!' he advised.

She knew this was true but, gritting her teeth, she copied. Very slowly, ignoring the shrieking muscles, she found he had been correct. The movements oiled the muscles, stretching them again, and gradually pain receded.

'That was—awful!' she told him with considerable feeling.

'We'll cut across country for a bit,' he said, and turned to lead the way, which took them through meadowland.

'Wild?' she asked bluntly.

He flared his nostrils, as his expression changed. 'Yes—him!' For a few seconds he rode without speaking, sorting out what could and could not be related. She must be put on her guard. Yet he did not wish to frighten her. Then a thought occurred to him. From yesterday's events it seemed she was a girl who would not frighten easily. She was simply too gutsy.

Anne waited and looked ahead, her own thoughts confused. He seemed to have sunk into one of his dour moods, showing the side of him that she did not like. Her mind switched track. Was it only two days ago she had been a bullied servant? Yesterday he had raped her. Last night and this morning, he could not have been kinder or more thoughtful. She fidgeted uneasily. She was not used to people who could switch characters so effortlessly, and she wasn't sure she liked this. It crossed her mind to wonder if he were a liar. Had he meant it, inviting her to be his guest? Was it possible he had some weird, ulterior motive that escaped her? Her mind flickered back to his mysterious nightly companion, and she began to puzzle it out. A highwayman must have an accomplice—yet, who could this be in her old area?

'Penny for your thoughts!' he said abruptly, and she glanced over at him, striving to show an impassive face. She had a sudden instinct that it would be imprudent to let him know everything. He was too sharply intelligent, too much of an unknown quantity. For her own safety, reticence would be prudent at all times. She would have been amazed to know that his thoughts mirrored hers.

Her muscles were fluid again, and she revelled in the pleasure of riding a well-bred horse. How wonderful it must be to have money, position and rank. Then the thought struck her that she was on a stolen horse, and her lips twitched with amusement. Why wasn't she shocked any more? Was it because this man, riding alongside, was a natural rebel and a law unto himself?

'Wake up!' he told her. 'You are daydreaming!' Or was she planning something nefarious, because of the rape? This one he must watch like a hawk.

'Wild?' she prompted.

'Yes,' he began slowly. 'Mr Jonathan Wild, born in Wolverhampton, father a wigmaker, but with a son who had no intention of copying his sire in life. What exactly happened no one knows except Wild himself, but he ended up in Wood Street Prison for debt. While there, he obviously made many contacts, and especially with one particular woman. When he left prison, she went with him, and together they opened a brothel in Lewkenor's Lane, and after a while they opened a public house in Cripplegate, London.'

He paused a moment. Much as he hated Wild, he could not but help admire him. 'Wild is bold, and also cruel. He is ambitious, wealthy and avaricious. He even blackmails thieves, and it takes a very hard man to do that in the first place. He bought goods, which thieves brought to him, then, cunning devil, found out from whom they had been stolen, and let the owners know he had them. To cap it all, he would up the price and the owners used to bid even higher to get their own goods back!'

Anne was staggered. 'But didn't people realise what was going on?'

Richard nodded wryly. 'They certainly did, because thieves thrive in the city, so a law was passed by which receivers were also made accessories. Did this stop Wild? Not a bit of it, he just went ahead and opened a house for the recovery of lost property as only he dared call it! He would then take a fee for making an enquiry about the lost property. After a suitable delay, just enough to turn the owner into a gibbering wreck, he would let them know he might be able to recover their goods. Always of course, for an appropriate and high recovery fee. He did so well at this, he moved into larger premises and started to steal on a commercial scale with roving gangs as paid operators. Each gang had a specific region to cover. One would operate the main roads from London. Another would deal with church thefts. A third would cover the centres of entertainment, while there was even a fourth for servants. Not long ago, Mr Wild branched out and purchased a sloop, so goods could be sailed to the continent.'

Anne thought about this. 'Goods—which people dare not reclaim if they had obtained them illegally in the first place?'

'Exactly!' he replied, and his eyebrows lifted.This girl was very sharp indeed. Was she too quick on the uptake for her own good?

'You have told me what Mr Wild does. But what kind of a man is he personally?' She was astounded at the story. Who would have thought such goings-on were part of life in the capital? What a tame, naive life she had lived in the country.

Richard considered this question, and did not reply immediately. Males and females were inclined to have opposite points of view at times.

'Outwardly, he is a pillar of respectability. Inwardly he is a snake. Many people consider him beneficial, and even an instrument of justice.'

'What! How can that be?'

'Simple!' he replied shortly. 'In his way he does keep crime under control. Albeit, his control! Anyhow, there has always been a shortage of men who dared testify against him. You see, Wild is a fair man for those who work for him, as long as they play by his rules. Those who remain loyal, with closed lips, want for nothing. God help those who go against him. He is without mercy. So you see, in a macabre way, he keeps the criminal fraternity under control. Perhaps also it is a case of better the devil you know than the one you don't know.'

Anne was speechless, hardly able to take this in. Her expression showed her bewilderment.

Richard continued remorselessly. 'If any fool does cross Wild he simply gets them convicted by paying witnesses to appear against the man.'

'That's terrible!' Anne cried aghast.

'Wild has had many innocents convicted to suit his own ends. But, to be fair, many bestial murderers have been brought to justice by him, without thought of benefit. Wild cleans trouble up. What I'm saying, I suppose, is that only a fool crosses him. He has the most incredible memory, and never forgets even the tiniest slight. He will wait years to take revenge then, out of the blue, he strikes'

'How?'

Richard paused before he continued, 'I'll give you an example. If one of Wild's gang goes on trial, and there is someone else around who has upset Wild, a third-party will swear Queen's evidence and the innocent man gets convicted, while the Wild's man gets a pardon.'

Richard stopped his horse and Anne

copied. 'Never cross Wild. Never talk about him either!'

Anne tilted her head and looked at him shrewdly. 'You hate him!' she said in a low voice. 'So why work for him?'

He gave a tiny shake to his head. 'Any highwayman can steal if he has the nous and guts. But how does he dispose of the goods? Wild has the market. I take to Wild what I acquire, he shifts it and gives me a percentage. I then pay him back another fee for his trouble.'

Anne eyed the stolen horse. Would the proceeds here go via Wild, or was Richard playing his own deadly game?

'How did you get involved in the first place?'

He grimaced. 'I was nearly caught trying to sell a gold brooch. It happened to be in my early days, and only a very fast horse saved me. After that, I decided it was safer and cheaper to deal with Wild.'

Anne gave a rapid snort. 'From what you have said, it seems to me this was a ploy on Mr Wild's part just to drive you into his fold!'

Richard caught his breath with awe. Who else would have worked this out so swiftly? He saw her lip curling with distaste, then her eyes narrowed and rested on him again with a probing question.

'Can't you break away from this man now?' she asked rapidly.

'Impossible!' he lied smoothly. 'Others have tried that before me.

'What happened to them?'

'They died,' he replied bluntly. 'Do remember the information now in your head is enough to put your own life in danger, should you say one word. Don't think because you are female Wild would have pity for you' He worded that carefully.

Anne gulped. He spoke the truth. ' I'll keep my mouth shut. I always have!'

Now, he recognised truth when he heard it, and his respect rose another notch. He gave a tiny nod to himself, missed by Anne. Perhaps, he mused, she will be useful after all.

Anne suddenly changed the subject. He had related so much she knew she would wish to think about this at night when alone. 'What is London really like?'

He too was thankful to change the conversation. 'It is a beautiful place for the rich and a hellhole for the poor. There are areas where I would not wander without a man to protect my back. See: we will ride over there and then be on the main route to the capital. Wise people do not dilly-dally. If they start late, they run the risk of being caught behind a pack train. The only way then is by taking a detour. If the pack train has come up from the coast, like Lyme Regis, it moves very fast indeed, with special trotting horses. It carries fish, and the idea is to get it to London and sold before it rots. Sometimes, coal travels that way too, if there is no suitable river. Always get out of the way of a pack train or right ahead of it.'

'Where do you get your information?' she asked him suddenly.

For a moment he did not like this question, as he put the wrong interpretation on it before he understood her angle. She meant his highwayman's activities.

'I frequent a lot of the coffee houses. I travel around all of them, picking up a snippet here and another there. Sometimes it's better at Beau Mondes at the White Chocolate House in St James Street. That's where the Whigs go. On the other hand, I might saunter into the Tory stronghold of the Cocoa Tree Chocolate House. Now and again I'll drop into Wills and Trubys'

'All of them?'

He threw her another of his lean, wolfish grins. 'It pays to when information is required.'

They breasted a slope and halted their horses. He pointed to where smoke rose as a thick cloud. 'London!'

Anne felt excitement to stir. So that was the place where life was lived to the full, and she would now be part of it. Then a new thought hit her, and her expression changed to one of doubt.

'What is it?'

'How will your servants view me?' she asked

nervously.

He frowned, for once being obtuse, but, aware of her eyes now large and worried, it hit him.

'They will view you as my guest or answer to me,' he stated firmly, then knew he must expand. 'My important and senior staff are: William my personal man, and Jenny my housekeeper. She is the next most important person to William and carries an acid tongue. They clash, but I never interfere as long as my home is run properly. Jenny is fifty years old, just a little younger than William. You would think their ages would make them friends but not a bit of it. They cannot stand each other. Jenny spits and snarls at William, while he would like me to get rid of her, which I won't because she's good at her job. There's Dan Copes who is twenty-one and works in the stables under William. We have a lad called Joe Hammond, who is coming along nicely, and he also obeys William. In the house, Jenny has Mary Bates, to help her with the heavy work and young Katie, who is sixteen. I know Jenny engages other staff as and when they are needed. Most of the staff came with the house except William who has been with me for more years than I care to remember. When I am away, William stands in as master, no matter what Jenny might think!' He looked at her seriously. 'Always remember the information in your head could also be your death warrant!'

Anne nodded very soberly. She realised she was about to enter the unknown and as much as the idea of living in London thrilled her, she was aware of her ignorance and naïveté. On top of this was the knowledge of this man's weird and dangerous life. She wanted her revenge on him, and now she had the information to provide this. She asked herself honestly did she really wish to act hastily? Surely it would be better to stretch her wings and have some fun first.

FIVE

A middle-aged man in brown, working breeches and a shabby fawn shirt clumped from the stalls and halted with surprise. He lifted his eyebrows as a smile of delight broke over a craggy face, which required a shave.

'Master!' he exclaimed. 'I wasn't expecting you just yet!' He greeted Richard with pleasure, then his smile vanished as his eyes landed on Anne. She saw perplexity enter dark brown eyes, which scanned her from head to boots, then turned an inquiring look upon Richard.

The younger man hastily cleared his throat, waved a hand a little half-heartedly and flashed some kind of look from his eyes. 'Hello

William!' he said clamping the other's outstretched hand in a brief shake. 'This lady is with me and we are both tired.'

William Chambers, frowned uncertainly. Lady? That seemed a charitable description, because already his sharp eyes had noted the rough hands that the young girl held before her on the reins. She looked back at him nervously, but his stare was direct and unflinching.

'Who is she?' he hissed at Richard.

Anne half turned, pretending to be disinterested, though this was far from the case. Her hearing had always been particularly acute, and though the men lowered their voices she managed to hear a few sentences.

'She's from Gloucestershire,' Richard whispered. He was aware Anne stood nearby, and she appeared to be examining his house with great interest but it crossed his mind to wonder whether she could hear them. Surely not?

'What!' William gasped. 'You're mad, Master!'

Richard took a deep breath. He sensed William was on the verge of turning difficult. 'I had no choice. It was bring her or kill her!' he hissed.

William snorted. 'Better the latter under the circumstances!' he said coldly. 'The last person we want here is someone from outside!'

'We'll discuss it later!' Richard told him.

Here and now was neither the time nor the place for an argument with his man, because on William's face was a look of obduracy.

Richard turned to Anne and threw her a smile. 'She will be my guest and young Katie can wait upon her as her maid. Welcome her!' he whispered, and the last two words were a cross between a plea and an order.

William gave another sniff and stared Anne back as she faced him. 'Welcome!' he said, lying in his teeth.

Anne recognised the lie and her hackles rose as quickly as her heart sank. For some reason, he hated her already—what was that about she should have been killed? Her blood had chilled at the tone in which the words had been uttered. They were callous, indifferent to her existence, and Richard had seemingly pleaded with the older man. What kind of household was this where the master had to ask his servant? Unease filled her rapidly. Had she done the wrong thing coming with him?

She gave a polite bob to her head, forced a thin smile upon her face and said, 'Thank you!' and managed to keep the sarcasm from her tone.

'Master!' a female voice cried next as a rear door opened and a woman saw them. She was stout, also middle-aged, with huge breasts and a scarlet face with straggly hair turning deep grey. Anne guessed this had to be Jenny who hurried over the cobbled yard, and ducked her head politely before throwing a glare at William.

'You are back early?' she asked.

'Yes!' Richard agreed pleasantly as Anne stood to one side. William had turned away in an obvious huff and stamped back into his stable region. The housekeeper gave her full attention to the female newcomer.

'This is Miss Howard who will be staying with me as my guest,' Richard said firmly.

Flecked green eyes turned to Anne, and again she knew she was scrutinised from head to toe. Jenny Huggins folded her arms before her very ample bosom as her lips twitched in disbelief. Her white apron crackled with its stiffener, and she breathed heavily and, as Anne regarded her in turn, she saw flour from wrists to elbows with a dusting on the fringe of a long, dark blue gown. She flushed with embarrassment at being examined as if she were farm produce for sale on the market stall.

'Miss Howard is to have the large room at the rear and young Katie is to attend to her needs!' And this time there was no mistaking a direct order.

Richard was sensitive enough to understand her present emotions. Anne was filled with unease and shyness. He narrowed his eyes thoughtfully, saw that hers had turned grey and worry filled him. Surely she could not have overheard William's tactless remark? His lips went a little tight. Was she one of these people with an uncanny hearing? It was obvious she would have felt William's antagonism, which meant there was a thundering row looming between him and his man. He had not failed to notice the surprise on his housekeeper's face. And of course she would instinctively categorise her as being no quality lady. He really would have to get something done to those dreadful hands, which gave her away at first glance.

'Jenny will take you to your room,' he told her gently and squeezed her right hand, 'then Katie will cone to you.'

Anne swallowed. 'And you?' she asked uncertainly.

'I have to go out,' he told her quietly, narrowing his eyes to stare directly into hers. 'This is my life!' he added quietly. 'I am a busy businessman—remember?'

Anne nodded and played along with him. Her heart fell at the thought she was going to be left alone with all these strangers, one of who already detested her presence. She regarded the housekeeper uneasily too. Was it her imagination, or did Jenny resent her as well? Certainly, there was no smile of welcome on the fat, slightly perspiring face, yet, how could the master's order be disobeyed? As she had also been a servant she was aware there were many ways in which a servant could irritate another's life. Please don't dislike me, she prayed silently but her instinct warned her this was already too late. For some reason, Jenny Huggins and William Chambers both felt the same about her. What is wrong with me, she asked herself wildly? If Katie was to be the third person and her heart plummeted miserably—she would never stay in a house with so much dislike. There had been too much of that at the farm.Yet, how could she leave? Where could she go? All she had was Lady Sarah's sovereign. And, worst question of all, what if he had made her pregnant? She was trapped in this house for at least another two weeks. She stiffened. Jenny would not browbeat her, and, lifting her chin pugnaciously, she outstared the older woman coolly. Jenny took the hint, as the master vanished into the stables for another of those get-togethers with that odious William.

'Come missy!' she managed to get out at last. 'I'll show you the room Master says you are to have—while you are here.'

Anne ignored the questioning innuendo and followed with dignity. She was taken along a corridor, up some stairs, and along another passage before Jenny finally opened a door, and stepped into a large chamber with Anne at her heels.

'This was the room Master has given to you and I'll send the girl up to you with hot water and food and drink. I expect Master will see to suitable clothes for you,' she said, showing disdain for what Anne wore.

Anne knew she had gone red, but she refused to drop her eyes before the housekeeper.

Jenny faced her. 'I'm in charge here, and I'm the one keeps the place running smoothly!' she stated pompously. 'Without me, this house will go to compete rack and ruin. I attend to all the master's needs and see he eats properly when he is home. That William thinks he is the be-all and end-all of existence here, but he's not!' she stated, hands clasped before her fat abdomen, as her voice rang with proprietary pride.

Anne felt a sharp giggle rise and struggled to smother it at birth. Jenny's pomposity was almost farcical, yet she knew to laugh would only make matters worse. The older woman objected to her presence, but she was not quite as openly hostile as William—yet, Anne added to herself.

Jenny Huggins was temporarily baffled. Young females had been brought into the house before for the master's bed, but they rarely stayed more than two or three days and William handled such matters. Jenny had no objections, and she already sensed William was put out by this girl's arrival, and presumed it was because the master had made his own arrangements for once. That would serve bossy William right, she thought with pleasure, delighted to know he had been taken down a peg or two.

Jenny let her eyes roam over the girl for a second time, quite aware such a detailed scrutiny was rude and embarrassing. She had assessed the newcomer's age as well as her past occupation. This one had spent years at menial labour. So why should the master put her in his best room and announce she was a guest? It was baffling and upsetting. On the other hand, Jenny sensed this girl was different. She did not stand with lowered head. If anything, the housekeeper saw cold, grey eyes, hard as flint stones with pinched nostrils and a defiantly tilted young head. Was it possible this servant girl held some importance for the master? It seemed odd but masters were laws unto themselves in their homes and lives. Who was she to object, except that Jenny considered the house her domain to rule, and she would brook no interference from any other female, let alone a serving wench. Did Missy here think she would take over the household reins? Over my dead body, Jenny told herself acidly. Start as you intend to go on had always been a good, steadfast motto, and now was as good a time as any.

Anne wondered how much longer, they were both going to stand like two stiff pieces of moulded clay. She sensed the older woman's attitude and decided attack was the best form of defence.

'Thank you,' she said politely. 'That'll be all for now!'

71

Jenny nearly gobbled at this dismissal. She swelled with indignation, gasped and bridled. The chit of a female had just dismissed her as a nonentity! She turned on her heels, lips a thin, tight line of outrage and stamped away. She shut the door pointedly with a louder bang than was quite necessary.

'Bitch!' Anne said to the room as her shoulders slumped. 'And troublemaker too!' For some reason totally unknown to her, she knew she had acquired two enemies. Miserably, she sank down on the edge of the bed, sitting on a gaiety coloured comforter and studied the room. It was enormous to her. There was a large leather chair, which looked comfortable and well used. On the opposite wall stood a desk with thin spindly legs. There was a great oak wardrobe placed against the third wall, which had carved doors with many spirals and twists, and, Anne noted, there was no dust anywhere. At least she had to admit Jenny was obviously highly efficient at her job.

She stood up and opened the wardrobe, her eyebrows going up at the sight of two gowns which hung there. One was light grey, and the other a deep fawn. Well, well! Who owned these, and what had happened to her? The floor had a proper carpet, which was a novelty to her, and she slipped off her uncouth boots. Would Richard let her get some new dainty ones?

There was a light tap at the door, which

made her jump, then it was opened and a young girl appeared with a jug of steaming water. She threw Anne a quick curtsy, placed the jug down on a shelf, which held the washing bowl, then quickly scurried away.

Anne refreshed herself, flung the soiled, torn gown in a corner, eyed the two on offer and selected the grey one. It was little on the small side, so she picked a seam open with a broken fingernail and slipped it on. Finally, she peeped curiously, through the shutters trying to make out details in the evening gloom.

Noises reached her ears. They were rattles from wheels on cobbles, and the clatter of hooves outside on the streets of London. From this house rose muted talk, then her attention turned to the stables. They appeared to be quiet and she guessed evening stables had already taken place.

'What am I doing here?' she asked herself again, sinking into the deep leather chair. She felt distinctly uneasy, sharply aware there was a deadly mystery about Richard Mason. Even allowing for the fact of his method of work using theft, this house, which had looked so magnificent at first glance, now appeared to carry a heavy aura of something frightening.

There was another sharp rap before the door opened and once more the maid appeared with a tray of food and drink.

'I was told to bring you this,' she said

timidly. 'Master has gone out, but said to tell you he'd see you upon his return.'

'Where did he go?'

'I don't know, ma'am. Master and William often go away or spend a lot of time together talking 'cos William is Master's man and very important to him. They are quite firm friends really,' and Katie blushed at her temerity.

'I know you are Katie, but from where?' Anne asked conversationally, trying to break the other's reserve so she could pick up information.

'From the orphanage, ma'am. I came to work here when I was eight years old and I have been here ever since,' Katie replied. Then dared to lift her gaze and throw a proper peep at this newcomer.

Katie was frightened as well as shy. On past occasions when the master had females stay she had not liked it. Two of them had been nice to her when the master was around but nasty as soon as his back had turned. They had pinched and bullied her. Another was free with her hands, slapping her face at the slightest excuse for slowness or other imagined misdemeanours.

She was under no illusions about her place in life. She was at the very end of the pecking order of life, as the orphanage had made perfectly clear. Although she had been glad to leave them to go out to work for her keep and a few pennies, there were not many happy days to counterbalance the bad ones. She was thankful for a roof over her head, a private attic chamber, and plenty of food to eat.

The master terrified her. He was so tall and strong, and she was overanxious to please him. Her greatest dread was he would find fault and send her away into an even worse unknown. Deep down, she doted upon him like a puppy before a new stern owner. Her upbringing had taught her she would never amount to anything of consequence and had been born to serve until the end of life.

This new guest terrified her. Would her bare arms be pinched again? Would she be slapped if she was slow or failed to understand something? She swallowed with trepidation and lowered her eyes again. It was the usually the safest place to have them.

'What is your last name?' Anne asked quietly. She examined the plain-faced girl and recognised fear when she saw it. This girl was terrified of her. What went on in this house that could so scare a young girl?

'Don't have one, ma'am! No one knows who I am. I was found abandoned as a new baby,' she whispered with fresh worry. Would this make any difference?

'Do you like it here?' Anne asked next.

Katie was so surprised that she lifted her gaze before nodding. 'Oh yes, ma'am! I am always warmly clothed, and well fed and Jenny doesn't hit me too much, though she has an awful tongue on her at times. Master is quiet and does not bother me in any way at all.'

Anne's eyebrows elevated. She guessed the girl did not have a disingenuous hair on her body. So Richard never took her to his bed. Was that charity, manners, consideration for his servants, or plain distaste?

'How long have you been here?'

Katie bit her lip and started to count on her fingers. 'It will be eight years come Christmas,' she said, 'but I have only been with this master the two years.'

Anne nodded to herself. That was one particle of useful information, which she stored in her mind for re-examination at a later time. She flashed a warm smile at the maid who stood uncomfortably and ill at ease.

Katie wondered if she dared relax. This guest did not appear to be like previous ones, and she felt herself start to thaw.

' Mistress Jenny has been here a long time, but not William,' she explained, feeling Anne's interest. Suddenly, she giggled, half covering her mouth. 'But you should hear Master and William argue at times. They always make up afterwards, though. Mistress Jenny and William row as well, though it is never William who starts it. Jenny likes to pick on him. I think she is jealous because of Master's closeness to William. Jenny would like to look after Master all by herself. She makes lovely food though, and Master always praises her and then William goes all quiet and sulks!'

Anne smiled encouragingly, but picked her words with care. 'What does the master do when he goes out or away?' she asked casually.

Katie shrugged. She was disinterested. 'I don't know, ma'am. He is away an awful lot, but when he is in London he spends many hours in the coffee houses. I have heard Jenny saying he must be making business investments.'

That tallied with what Richard had told her and she nearly giggled too. He was certainly seeing to his business interests, she thought merrily, then pulled her features sober again.

'Will that be all, ma'am?'

Anne leaned forward, urgently to hold the maid's complete attention. 'I am a stranger here in London,' she began softly. 'I am only used to living in the country, and I think I am going to find the capital very strange for quite a while. I do hope we can be friends?'

Now it was Katie's turn to go scarlet with embarrassment. No one had ever asked for her friendship before, and she had no idea how to react. This lady was Master's guest so how could they be friends? With a nervous bob she turned and fled with fear at this weird request.

Anne grimaced and rebuked herself. She had moved far too quickly, and too soon. Timid Katie needed to be wooed with kindness, which required time, she thought. It was night now and she felt great weariness, so looked thoughtfully at the comfortable bed.

There was a third knock, and she had to open the door. He stepped in, throwing her a grin. 'Good!' Richard said evenly. He had just had a thundering row with William but long ago he had learned to push such matters to the back of his head in readiness for the next step. 'Sorry I couldn't come before, but I was busy.' He took one of her hands and looked down at her. 'Friends?' he asked gently.

Anne thought how wonderful he was when he was in this softer mood. 'Well, why not?' she replied in a low voice.

He sat down on the edge of the bed and grinned at her like a little boy. 'Now,' he began briskly, 'I will have to be away for a few days unfortunately.'

Anne raised her eyebrows. Stealing, she wanted to ask, but decided not to. She wanted to keep him in this gay mood. 'I've arranged for you to have reading material when I am not here. Regular copies of the *New Spectator* and the *Tatler* will come for your exclusive use. At the moment there's not a lot else available, because the press law has put a penny tax on anything the government thinks a news sheet.'

Anne beamed, pleased with his swift arrangements. It seemed he was a man of his word, then puckered her forehead. There was a matter that she must raise.

'What is it?' he asked quickly.

Anne stared back at him intently. 'I am used

to the open air and countryside. The idea of being confined in this house—' and she waved her right hand expressively. 'I think it would soon drive me crazy!'

Richard nodded. What she said made sense. 'William will escort you out riding, or one of the lads, and Katie can go with you walking.'

She smiled, pleased with him, then threw him an arch look. 'Who is William?'

He paused a moment. 'William is the linchpin of my household. He has been with me as far back as I can remember. He was a young friend of my father, whom I cannot remember at all. When my father was killed in a fight, it was William who looked after me. He saw I had a proper education. He taught me to ride, fence and shoot. He made a man of me and I owe more to William than words can hope to express. All through those years he kept us and some female servants by winning at dice. William is completely trustworthy, totally loyal to me and my very best friend.'

Anne did not miss the affection in his voice plus something else. A definite hint that more questions would get her nowhere as William was none of her business. He answered only to the master of the household.

'Is he gentry?' she asked quietly. It was important, she learned what made William tick as he had shown such instant dislike for her.

Richard's shoulders moved noncommittally. 'I think he was years ago, when I was a little, but he fell upon hard times, which was why he turned to gambling. He has never told me about any family he might have had. I did ask once and was firmly told to mind my own business,' he told her ruefully. 'I never asked a second time. I take William for who he is. An incredible man, whom I love as an older, big brother.'

He paused, a reflective smile on his face, and Anne kept quiet. He really was most handsome, when in this benign frame of mind.

'William is a deep man, and I always felt it wrong to probe. Anyhow, I respect him far too much for that. Now,' he said changing the subject, 'I have some excellent hacks here, and even side saddles, though I expect you would scorn these? I thought so, but you will certainly raise a few eyebrows, riding astride like a man. However, that bothers me not one jot. I have told William you are competent, though I don't think he quite believes me!'

Anne went alert at that. Why did her instinct warn her she was due to clash with William as well, as with Jenny, which knowledge made her a heart sink a little. She knew she could not mention this. He might throw a construction upon such observation in that she was a born troublemaker. Then a fresh thought entered her head, and she looked down at the pair of slippers she had discovered in the wardrobe.

He thought he anticipated her hesitancy.

'Clothes!' he said briskly. 'And better footwear! I'll order Katie to take you out to make a selection. We can't have you looking like a rustic in London!' he teased, then he reached over and took one of her hands. 'These too! I am sure Katie will know the tricks to soften your hands with hot water and goose grease at night. By the time she has finished you'll match all the ladies!'

Anne threw him a droll look of disbelief. It would be nice to think that, but she knew better. It was true, fine clothes and soft hands would transform her, but surely they could make no alteration to the true individual. It would be exciting to dress nicely and wear soft footwear, and her cheeks flushed at this thought, then her expression gloomed again. Now she felt almost too embarrassed to mention another request. He was being very generous; he might think her greedy.

'What is it?' he whispered, puzzled once again. What a complicated girl she was. Most would be dancing with joy at the prospect of a brand new wardrobe, yet she still sat subdued. There was something else she wanted, and his heart swelled. He would be delighted to get it for her if it were within his power. For a second, he wondered at his own strange emotions but forced them aside. He told himself he was just being charitable to a less well off guest.

Anne felt horribly nervous, then decided to

be bold, as she had nothing to lose.

'I have never had anything of value of my own,' she began slowly. 'There is something I have always wanted. Something that will be my very own, which I would treasure. There was never the slightest hope when I lived in Yate. So I didn't want to think about it too much. Now though—' She paused to see how he was reacting, holding her breath with nerves.

Richard stood up, bent forward. Her face turned upwards to him, and it was bleak and deadly serious while agitation flashed in her eyes and she quivered from nervous apprehension.

'What is it? A piece of jewellery? A diamond brooch? A special fur?'

She shook her head briskly. 'My own horse!'

He was startled, almost thunderstruck. Of all the objects a female might request, this one would never have crossed his mind in a dozen years. He could see wistful pathos in her eyes and was uncertain whether they were pale blue or grey, but they glowed with the fervent desire to own and possess.

'A horse,' he echoed with astonishment. 'Do you know enough to pick a good one?'

Anne nodded and started to beam, a hopeful smile. 'My old master saw to that!'

He grinned. If her equestrian knowledge equalled her riding ability she would certainly know a good horse from a bad one.

'You can have any horse in my stables,

except two which I alone ride. That brown and another like him, who has two long white stockings. I'll tell William. That animal you rode goes in the morning for sale a long way from here so forget him!' He grinned wolfishly at her. 'The horse you pick will become your own personal property, and I'll put it in writing for you!' he told her.

The pleasure that flooded her face made his own heart swell. The gift was so little to him, who had always been well horsed. Anne laughed happily, then halted abruptly as something occurred to her.

'Are any of them—?'

He guffawed. 'No! All the horses in my yard, except that which goes tomorrow, are safe. I actually bought them!' he chuckled.

Anne pulled her hands away, stood up, twirled on her toes and clapped her hands with glee. The delight and happiness on her face touched his core.

'I will be away for a few days, so you can examine the horses and pick one for yourself. William might be away for a couple of nights and Dan will be in charge. Wait until I am back though,' and she recognised an order when she heard one. She nodded, impressed by his words. She guessed his absence was connected with his highwayman activities, and it seemed as if William was involved as well. 'While I am away go out with Katie, but do not wander into doubtful areas. She will know the safe streets.

You know something, Anne Howard? I am very glad you are here!'

*   *   *

William seethed. He had been taken aback by the girl's arrival and when Richard had given him the details his anger had arisen until they had been involved in a furious row. He knew it would all blow over, but the girl would not. Richard insisted she was to stay for a while, yet when questioned there appeared to be no time limit.

His anger went deep and arose from their situation in general. For once, he was lost as to what he should do. He was also honest enough to admit that his first impression of the girl was not a good one. She seemed to have a little more bold spirit than he liked in a young female, which boded ill. He had been thoroughly put out with the way she had stared at him instead of lowering her gaze meekly. Her eyes had been just a little too steady and probing. There was also something else, which niggled at him when he considered the girl's presence, and it was about this to which he was slowly coming to a conclusion. He would have to act. There was a bad enough atmosphere in the house with that hot-tempered Jenny constantly trying to provoke him.

William growled under his breath, feeling thoroughly bad-tempered himself just because

84

of the current domestic situation. He stared at the line of horses, all neatly tied with chains to their head collars.There was something hypnotically soothing in listening to horses eat. Their teeth ground rhythmically, which made a sound to lull a person's emotions.

Although he watched Dan and Joe putting down the fresh straw for night his mind was still on the girl. The Master's guest, indeed! Who did he think he was fooling? Although the master gave the orders, and his private life was supposed to be his own, everyone connected with him was, to a certain extent, affected by his actions. William frowned with heavy concentration.

Dan came out of a stall, saw him and his heavy frown and tactfully retreated, flashing a warning look at Joe.

'What is it?' Joe hissed, replacing a pitchfork in its holder.

'He is wearing his thundercloud look!' Dan warned.

Joe flinched. 'I'm keeping out of his way then!'

William's gaze lifted and he caught them talking. 'Here! Get out with your work and stop chatting like girls!' he snapped, then rebuked himself. He was taking his temper out on the boys, which was grossly unfair. It was true that young Joe had to have a kick in his breeches at times, but Dan was a fine young man, and completely responsible. On more than one occasion, he had noticed Dan's eyes rest on Katie with more than usual interest. Was it possible something brewed in that direction? If so, he approved. They would make a good match, if only Katie could emerge from her shell a little, though how that could happen when she was under Jenny's thumb was questionable.

SIX

They faced each other and of the two Anne was the more disconcerted. She had risen early, quickly broken her fast, then discovered William was back, although Richard was not. During the two men's absence she had spent considerable time in the stable block; not only getting to know Dan and Joe but, far more important in her eyes, estimating the horses.

Now the day had to come to pick one for herself and she bubbled with excitement, though this had been tinged with worry. She would have to deal with grumpy William. She had debated waiting for Richard's return, but the thrill of imminent ownership had encouraged her to beard the lion in his den after all. The trouble was, she suspected, William was as touchy about the stable's area as Jenny was regarding her kitchen domain.

William had awoken in a thoroughly bad

mood brought about by what he now knew. As if he and the master did not have enough problems without an extra one, which, William suspected, would be lumbered most of the time on his back. After eating a silent breakfast he had come into the stables, growled at Dan, shouted at Joe then turned to be confronted by the girl. She had entered his private realm without as much as even a by-your-leave. His temper had shot up accordingly, fuelled by a look on the girl's face, which was set firm and unyielding.

'What do you want?' he growled at her. He was livid at this unwarranted territorial invasion.

Anne was swept by a nervous wave, then she pushed this firmly aside. She was not doing anything wrong. Richard had told her to pick a week after William returned.

'I've come to select my own horse. The master said I could when you returned. I've been making my selection all week!'

'Have you?' William grated. Impudent chit. As if she knew anything despite what Richard had said. Riding and selecting horses were not the same thing.

'I've made my choice too!' Anne continued. What an objectionable man this was. Anyone would think he was the master of this establishment, the way he behaved. No wonder Jenny did not like him, Anne reflected.

'What do you know about horses?'

Anne struggled to control her temper. 'I do know a little,' she said, striving to remain calm and act like a lady.

William was furious. The master had failed to mention this, which was inexcusable. This chit of a girl had been making free with his stables during his absence. No doubt gossiping to Dan and Joe, keeping them from their work. His anger rose higher. He would not tolerate this state of affairs, and now she dared to pontificate upon which animal she would have. He would see about that. The girl would not dare to lie so Richard had obviously given his consent but he, William, should have been informed.

'I'll take the black mare!' Anne told him firmly.

'What!' William bellowed. 'You'll do no such thing. That mare is not a female's ride!'

This was the final straw, because he knew, if anything did happen to the girl, it would be he who would have to bear the brunt of the master's wrath. This was exactly what happened when petticoat rule was not curtailed instantly.

Anne had examined each of the well-bred horses with great care, and also watched how they reacted to stable management with Dan and Joe. All of the horses' stalls were on the right-hand side of a long passage. On the left were the areas which housed the feed bins, the saddles and bridles. Overhead was a long loft in which was kept the hay and straw. These came down to the lower corridor through a long chute which, when not in use, could be fastened up out of the way. The loft's stairs stood at one end of the stalls' passageway. She had climbed these to poke her head through at the top to examine this area. All of the stabling bristled with cleanliness and smelt sweet and welcoming. Anne was very impressed with William's high standards, but had no intention of complimenting him.

'The black mare!' she repeated stubbornly.

'Certainly not!' William snapped back through tight lips.

'She's the best for me!' Anne argued hotly.

William hesitated fractionally at this statement. It was unfit, almost indecent, for a young girl to know about horses, although it was true. The black mare was a well bred, fast, fetching creature except for a wayward temperament. His face set in a mutinous glower.

'I said no!' he grated, terminating this ridiculous idea.

'But I say yes!' Anne retorted, her hackles bristling. He was trying to humiliate her by being awkward.

'Girl!' William thundered. 'You want your rear end beating hard!'

'Old man!' Anne hurled back at him. 'You want to learn a few manners for your master's guests!' She was almost frantic with anger and frightened she would lose the argument.

William swelled with wrath and his cheeks flamed with rage. This chit had gone too far now. Who did she think she was? No man dared to address him in such a tone, except his master. And he was *not* an old man either!

Anne stamped her right foot with frustration as she remembered all that which old Jacob had taught her. On one well remembered day, he had said, 'There's good and bad in horses. Sometimes a horse is bad through and through, though it is rare, and this has usually been caused by some ham-fisted, harsh man. You treat a horse with kindness and firmness, and he will respond to you, because the horse is a willing animal, given half a chance.'

Anne's heart had gone out to the black mare, who stood just over fifteen hands tall. She had studied carefully the mare's points, as other instructions from Jacob returned with clarity. 'Always look for a horse who is deep through the heart. Make sure he has a nice short back with large quarters. The head should be small, with eyes spaced far apart, and the whole set upon a proud neck. The legs must be clean and free from blemishes, especially around the hocks and cannon bones. The pasterns must be neither too short, nor too long. Small hooves are good, not big soup plates of feet, but the stride shall be that of a giant!'

The black mare fitted this description, as if she had been made for her. It was true, the mare's eyes rolled to flare white at Anne's slow approach, and her quarters bunched with apprehension. When Anne laid a gentle hand on the glossy neck the head turned and shining, anxious, liquid eyes locked into hers with a nervous question.

'Are you kind?' they asked.

'Yes, I am kind!' Anne had replied.

The mare inhaled the girl's scent and body aroma while Anne breathed back into flaring nostrils. Both animal and girl felt the rapport at the same time.

'She is an over-spirited and bad tempered mount!' William growled, between his teeth. 'She bucks, rears and bolts when she has a mind too!'

Anne threw him an acid look. 'I'm not surprised, if she has you to contend with!' she snapped, well aware she was now being very rude to an older person, but William's belligerent stance angered her anew.

'Why, you ill-mannered chit!' William gobbled with fury. 'I'll—I'll—!' and he lifted one great hand as rage spilled over.

Anne leaped backwards with youth's speed and grabbed a nearby pitchfork. She levelled its two vicious tines in the region of William's rather corpulent abdomen.

He froze instantly as he stared into blazing eyes. He swore to himself, and knew he had miscalculated badly. This girl meant business, and held the tool in a workmanlike manner, showing she had handled pitchforks before. Her face was a rigid mask, her teeth bared, and he almost swore she snarled like a treed cat.Very warily he shifted his body weight and retreated gingerly from the pitchfork's range limit.

'You—!' he started, then halted, unable for a moment to think of a suitable expletive.

Anne had sense enough not to follow, and over push her advantage. His retreat was her victory bought at the price though of his undying enmity. William turned and stomped angrily back down the passage.

Dan and Joe peeped down through the loft's open hatch, took one look at William's face, swallowed and sensibly decided to stay where they were until man and girl had long departed.

Dan was tall, though not yet fully developed, but he hinted at the big man he would become. He was quiet and thoughtful, delighting in his work and supremely happy at the Mason establishment but he too was distinctly uneasy about this weird girl. He had been in no position to bar her from her daily visits to the stables, and he had guessed what William's reaction would be.

Although it had often crossed Dan's mind he had enough experience to apply for a position under a better-tempered man than

William Chambers, he always hesitated because of Katie. He thought she was quite wonderful, everything his heart desired and he had been slowly working around to ask the maid to walk out with him.

Joe considered this a huge joke and teased him unmercifully. Mostly Dan took this in good part because of Joe's youth. In Joe's eyes, maids were playthings for healthy, lusty males like himself to enjoy, but they generally worked well together. William's discipline saw to that. Now both of them were thoroughly alarmed. William on the warpath was someone to be avoided. That girl must be quite insane.

'We'll stay up here. It'll be safer,' Dan hissed to Joe.

'You're right!' Joe whispered back, his face white What kind of a girl was this to threaten William?

Anne was left in solitary state, happily triumphant, but depressed in another. She felt in her bones Richard would not object when he learned what she had done. After all, William had intended to hit her!

The black mare nickered, so she replaced the fork and turned to the elegant black nose, then her lips tightened as she saw something fresh. The mare had been ridden since their last visit, and it was obvious why she had a bad reputation. She had fire and spirit, and William was consumed with pride and dominance so he must have used some long curb bit. There was a sore at the mare's mouth, enough to make even a placid horse fret.

'I think we are two of a kind!' she murmured and one ear twitched at her voice. 'I will ride you and you would let me because I shall use the most gentle snaffle bit. We will become friends,' she breathed, and the mare tossed her head up and down.

She heard steps coming back and stiffened warily. William reappeared carrying the two saddles, one under each arm. One of which was a side-saddle. They regarded each other balefully. Anne held her head high while William pointedly ignored her. Each waited for the other to speak first. Anne lapsed into the defensive silence that she had learned aggravated males, and William immediately took this to be mulish sulking.

Anne studied him. He was not as tall as Richard, but there was great depth to his chest, and he had huge shoulders. Massive muscles showed on his forearms, where he had rolled up his sleeves and for such a heavy man he moved quickly and lightly on his feet.

'My mare is to be called Night!' she said quietly, as if it were an aside. Someone had to speak first.

William turned slowly and eyed her up and down as if she were for sale. She had dared to threaten him. Him! Thank God, the stable boys were not around to have seen this disgraceful episode. He writhed with internal embarrassment and would certainly have something to say to the master when he returned.

Anne watched the wrath on his face and misconstrued fresh anger. William slapped a saddle on a mount, while Anne bit her lip as he turned to the mare with a side-saddle and a long curb bit.

'No!' she said with a coolness that she did not feel. 'A cross saddle and a snaffle bit!'

William's face turned redder with mortification and his lips tightened into such a thin line they almost disappeared. His chest swelled again and Anne stared, pop-eyed with fascination. William seemed to grow bigger and bigger. Surely he would explode in another minute?

'Get the tack and put it on yourself then!' William snarled, nearly completely out of control. He strolled away, swearing lustily at the female gender in general and her in particular.

Anne watched his stiff-legged strut, shrugged and walked to where the tack was kept. She was perfectly capable of all stable routine, but had no idea this was unheard of in London. She picked her selection and returned, to the interest of the mare, and talked gently to her, as she saddled up.

William watched from the corner of a window, his eyes wide with shock. The mare was correctly attired, led from the stall, and before his stunned gaze the girl had swung into the saddle with ease and grace. Thoroughly disconcerted, he fetched his own horse outside and mounted up.

They rode for a whole hour and exchanged not one word, though each kept surreptitiously, eyeing the other. Anne thought William rode solidly and lacked Richard's fluidity but he was secure in the saddle even if he did more demand of his horse than ride it.

He studied her.The master was right, the girl could certainly ride and sat astride like a man. He was lost for words, never having been in this position before in his life. The girl melded to the mare who, perversely, responded for her, as she never had for him. The fact the girl was right, and he had been proven wrong, did nothing to abate his temper.

He rode away from the congested areas and soon they were in open countryside, where they could canter and gallop. Anne was filled with glee. It was not just the sheer pleasure of riding a superbly bred horse, nor the wonder of knowing she was the owner. It was the delightful fact she was well away from the crowded hubbub of London in general.

The mare behaved impeccably to William's chagrin. She had good paces and was fast when asked to gallop. William knew few men who would be able to ride better than this girl and he was puzzled by her rare skill, but he was sufficiently old-fashioned to consider there was something not quite decent for a female to ride with her legs apart.

They walked back to the busy streets and clattered into the yard. William was still in a dour mood but Anne's cheeks were flushed with exhilaration, and her eyes sparkled with joy. He made no attempt to help her dismount, wanting to see if she could manage on her own.

Anne swung from the saddle briskly, jumping the last two feet to land neatly on her toes before she turned and looked up at him. She could not help the challenge in her eyes, and it was then that both acknowledged open war was officially declared.

With victory, she felt happier in the house. It was true, Jenny was horribly distant, forever watching her every move, so wisely Anne forbore to comment. She tried to be pleasant to the older woman, though instinct warned her there were storm clouds on the horizon.

For two days nothing happened. Anne rode out each morning, escorted by Dan, leaving Joe with a fit of the sulks, and, more to the point, under William's eagle eyes. She struggled to talk to Dan, but he was far too overawed by her prowess so she gave up on him, and simply enjoyed the pleasure of her mare.

Katie was confused. She waited upon the guest eagerly, striving to anticipate her every want. Material had been selected and new garments hastily made, with appropriate footwear. She worked hard on Anne's hands, gradually scraping away the awful calluses and, to Anne's delight, her large hands began to lose their work-worn appearance though she ruefully told herself she had a long way to go yet to display ladies' hands.

Her new wardrobe fascinated her with her skirts divided for riding purposes. She would pirouette before a long glass and Katie's admiring eyes.

Anne was a realist, because that was what life had taught her. Under these fine clothes she was still the very same person. She suddenly craved an audience. She yearned to show off all this finery. Where was Richard? He seemed to have been away a long time, and her blood chilled because obviously he must be out stealing with all the danger that entailed. She was almost happy except the one constant, which never left the back of her mind. Was she pregnant? She counted the days anxiously and realised she would soon know. If she were— but whenever her mind reached this point, her heart would flutter uneasily. Of course she could not trust Richard Mason, she told herself scolding. She must simply use him for whatever she could get from him. Why then did she miss him so much?

Katie was happy in one way, but apprehensive in another. This lady guest was a real talker. She chatted amicably and asked delicate questions, most of which she could not answer through ignorance. She knew little about horses, and nothing about the countryside. The affairs of the master were beyond her, and William was almost a god who scared Katie half to death just with his presence.

It was Jenny who was the fly in the ointment, because the housekeeper resented Katie's new position. She had become used to using the maid's services, rather than calling in outside help. An atmosphere started to develop, which worried Katie, because she had no idea what to do. Jenny would bristle silently whenever she saw Mistress Anne, and even glower behind her back.

It all came to a head one morning. Jenny had risen from her bed on the wrong side. Katie was half dreaming, because the previous evening Dan had thrown her two beaming smiles and asked her to take a walk out with him on her next free-time.

Anne sat in solitary state in the dining room as she broke her fast. Richard had thoughtfully left orders for her to have a dish of tea each morning, which she enjoyed. Jenny did not approve of such extravagance, but dared say nothing. She let her feelings be known by sotto voce grumbles, pitched just high enough for Anne to hear.

Katie waited on Anne, her face white with

worry, knowing Jenny's mood. Anne was engrossed in her own complicated thoughts, not really aware of Katie when she heard a sharp sound, which she knew only too well. It was followed by a gasp.

She was out of her chair in a flash, at the open door, and in the corridor before Jenny realised. The housekeeper had brought her arm back for a second blow, while Katie stood, left hand holding an inflamed cheek and tears trickling slowly.

Anne took in the scene and her mind flew back. How often had she been treated in like vein for some trifling offence! Her anger rose, swift and instinctive, as Jenny's arm began to move downwards. Before the hand reached its target, Anne grasped the arm.

Jenny was a strong woman, from years of lifting heavy pans with boiling contents from stove to tabletop but against Anne she was ineffectual. Anne's muscles had been tempered with years of very harsh labour and honed to a fine pitch from dealing with horses and other large animals. She was also fuelled by the injustice of the scene, which reminded her vividly of her own unhappiness without redress.

Jenny turned a furious face at Anne and strained her arm muscles. Anne simply tightened her grip and ruthlessly forced the housekeeper's arm back and upwards, while she held Jenny eyes in a cold, steady glower of direct challenge.

Jenny quailed. In the young girl's eyes was ice, and—something else. A hard, unmerciful defiance from a cold face with compressed lips and a belligerent jaw.

'If you fancy hitting someone—try me!' Anne challenged in a low tone, each word a brittle pistol shot of total contempt.

'Why you—!' Jenny blustered. 'I'm in charge here. I run this house, and I'll keep order as I see fit. I'll be speaking to the master about you!' she threatened wildly, badly humiliated, not quite knowing what to do about the situation.

Katie cringed with horror. How brave Miss Anne was, but now this would make her situation worse. She started to back in a panic.

'That will be two of us then!' Anne retorted evenly. 'Because I shall most certainly be letting him know my point of view about female bullies!'

'Well!' Jenny snorted, trying to cover up her genuine alarm with indignation. There was something a little frightening about the stranger. What was it young Joe had said had happened to William? She bit her lip, confused and now scared. Joe had said this missy had dared to threaten William with a pitchfork. She must be quite mad. They would all end up murdered in their beds. She wondered how she could retreat and save face. She gave a tentative tug with her arm, but it was still firmly anchored in a grip as strong as that of any man.

Anne's mind moved rapidly forward to see a way out of this impasse, which would save Katie, who was now crying copiously.

'Furthermore,' Anne continued in the same low, threatening voice, 'the Master said Katie was to wait upon me. From now on she will do that, all day and every day!'

'Impossible!' Jenny snapped. 'The girl has no time for such idleness. I have important work for her to do! Who do you think you are coming into this house and ordering faithful loyal servants about?' Jenny cried wildly, aware she was losing this battle very badly, and embarrassed before Katie.

'And who exactly are you to countermand the master's specific orders?' Anne retorted sweetly. She knew she had won but felt no delight in this. She now had enemy number two lined up against her, but she did not regret the stand she had taken. She was equally sure Richard would back her in this.

'Katie will be with me all day,' she repeated carefully, 'and when I have finished with her services she will be on our own free time. You must get outside help in or—' She paused, thinking. Should she administer the coup de grace? What did she have to lose? It would certainly clarify the situation once and for all. With a deep breath, she spoke again. 'Or is it you have such a bad, bullying reputation that servants don't want to come and work here under you?' she asked acidly.

'I have had enough!' Jenny cried. 'I'll leave!'

For a few seconds Anne was alarmed, but there was no going back. 'That's up to you!' she replied with a coolness she did not quite feel. 'You will then have to see the master about your references, won't you?' she remarked carefully and weighed in with narrowed eyes.

Now Jenny blanched. Although she knew she was superb at her work, references were vital to obtain a good position. Guilt dug its claws in her. She knew she did throw her weight around. It was a struggle to keep her temper under control but there was something quite implacable about this girl. The fact she was the master's private guest added fuel to her trepidation. She gulped, shook her arm and Anne released it. She stood a few seconds, rubbing where Anne's fingers had dug in, then turned and stormed back to the kitchen, slamming the door behind her.

Katie, opened her mouth to speak and gave a little start. Anne turned quickly and was shocked to see William standing there. How long had he been present? What had he overheard? She swallowed and faced him ready for his tirade. Her chin came up, and she bristled ready and alert.

William's good temper was suddenly restored. He had not missed a word, and privately approved. Anything that took Jenny down a notch or two was fine in his eyes. He also felt a stab of sheer admiration for what the girl had done. So his experience was not a sole one. This young girl had something inside her, which was all steel. She had a flaring spirit, with rare boldness. He was also glad at what she had done, because he too had not missed the times when Katie had worked with tearstained cheeks. He regarded Anne gravely. Her defiance was absolute, and he knew she was waiting for his condemnation as well.

'Good!' he grunted. 'That was long overdue!' he told her, then turned and walked away, completely forgetting what he had gone over to the house for in the first place. His good temper quite restored, he nodded to the boys affably before going to check the horses. Dan and Joe exchanged bewildered looks, then carried on with their work. Mistress Anne's arrival had been like an explosion in this establishment.

Katie wiped her face with the back of one hand. 'Oh ma'am!' she said in a low voice. 'You are brave!'

Anne turned to and smiled wearily. She felt enormously touched by what William had said, clutching at his approval like the drowning man with his straw. Did this mean he was no longer quite so hostile to her? She felt flutters of hope in her heart before turning her full attention to the maid.

'You don't mind?' she asked, then hastened to explain. 'Working just for me?'

'Oh no!' Katie breathed, clasping her hands together. 'I'd like that!' she paused. 'I would much rather be with you, ma'am. Jenny has always been free with her hands, and her tongue,' she confided.

'I can see that!' Anne told her grimly.

Katie paused, working out what she wanted to say next. Her tongue touched her lips hesitantly, and she plucked up courage to speak.

'I don't suppose you'll hit me or pinch like Master's other lady guests have done?' she asked timorously.

Anne gasped. 'No, I will not!' she said firmly. 'What other guests?'

Katy gave a little shrug. 'Other ladies the master had to stay now and again.'

'For how long?' Anne probed delicately.

Katie gave another little shrug. 'Never very long, two nights or three at the most!' she explained.

Anne considered this. 'Did they make repeat visits?'

Katie shook her head firmly. 'No, never!'

Anne thought about this. Just general bedwarmers, she told herself, so where does that leave me? What is going to happen when Richard finally returns? She wondered how she could learn more. So began to pick her words delicately.

'What type of ladies were they?' she asked with faked nonchalance.

Katie threw her a look. 'That kind, ma'am,' she replied then examined her new mistress. For a few seconds some of Anne's bold spirit rubbed off on her. 'Are you one of these ladies?'

Anne gasped, too shocked to be outraged, then her humour bubbled to the surface. 'Do I look like one?'

Katie shook her head firmly. 'Not at, all ma'am. You are so different to the others!'

'Thank God for that!' Anne said but more to herself. Of course Richard would have sexual companions, but me? Oh no, she vowed! Resolutely, she forced her thoughts back to Katie who still looked up at her, eyes shining with admiration. She almost felt like giggling, because Katie was regarding her with the adoration a young puppy has for its master. All she needed was a long tail to wag.

SEVEN

A few evenings later, she dropped off to a pleasant sleep. Her flow had started; she was not pregnant after all, and a great worry lifted from her mind. At the same time, though, she became aware of disappointment, which puzzled her. For a few seconds, she tried to picture what his baby would have been like. If a son, would he have inherited his powerful character? Would a daughter have turned out like her? She gave a rueful shake to her head. She knew only too well the vagaries of breeding stock. Even the best plans of men could never guarantee the foal or calf would turn out exactly as planned so why would it be any different with people?

She and Katie had been on a short walk that afternoon and she had tried to work out how long Richard had been absent. Although William was still a little distant with her he was certainly not as hostile since the morning she had bested Jenny.

Between Anne and Jenny was a tall barrier of ice, impenetrable and enormous, so Anne scrupulously kept right away from the kitchen area. She had no intention of putting herself in a position to give Jenny a legitimate complaint of trespass. She remembered only too well how Agnes had guarded her domain with fierce possessiveness. Only those who worked there entered without a specific invitation. Even a good master called the housekeeper to his study; he wouldn't dream of invading the kitchen region, which was always sacrosanct to the housekeeper.

She awoke with a start, some time in the night and lay still, puzzled as to what could have jabbed her senses alert. Anne lay rigid and strained her ears for a clue when she heard the particular sound. A second time she heard a floorboard creak with a tiny squeal right outside her door and she stilled with the shock. She stared at the door latch mesmerised, but it did not move. Without a second thought she slipped from her bed, pushed her feet into slippers and dived into a robe.

Anne eased the door open and peeped. A lantern bobbed ahead like a yellow ghost, and she frowned with bewilderment. Only William and Jenny had rooms on this floor at the far end, and then a second thought struck her. She slipped back into her room and peered through the window. She was sure she could see a shadow moving about restlessly at the mouth of the drive.

She bit her lip, hesitated, then moved. The dark figure had the silhouette of Richard and that lantern could only mean William was up and about. She considered swiftly, when it hit her. The obvious place for a secret, private conversation at this hour would be the stables.

She opened the door, and quickly pattered along the opposite way and down the other flight of stairs. Her heart palpitated wildly, and her throat had gone dry, but she knew she must eavesdrop. There were just too many weird questions about this house. Surely this was a God-given opportunity to learn what was going on?

Her quick eyes noted the door hinges had

been freshly greased and the door opened silently. She fled across the cobbles and around to the stables' rear door. She paused only a second, near the horses' passage and one animal moved restlessly, then she was up the stairs to the loft, just as the lantern beam showed at the entrance.

She nearly stumbled in the loft's gloom and halted to allow her eyes to adjust. The loft smelt sweetly of good seed hay and she blessed William's neat and tidy mind.

The hay was stacked on one side in sheaves with the straw on the other. In between, a natural passage had been left clear and down this she tiptoed like a wraith. When she estimated she was about halfway down she stopped and lowered herself to the slightly dusty floorboards. She had suddenly remembered there was a seat halfway. Surely this was where people would halt to talk?

There was slight crack and by placing her eye at this spot she was able to have limited vision. Voices rose in the night's stillness and Anne noted the horses did not move, nor stamp warning hooves. They knew the men and recognised William's voice. What was he up to?

'Well, Master! I'm glad to see you back!' and William's voice rang with relief.

So it *was* Richard!

'I'm sick of riding and talking. I'll not be sorry to have a rest.'

'I have news,' William growled. 'Gaultier is back!'

'What!' Richard said, startled, 'Good God! That can only mean one thing—!'

'I am afraid so!' William replied soberly.

'That explains it then!' Richard remarked slowly. 'I have been picking up an odd this and that. But I had not yet been able to bottom the rumours. Now I understand!'

Anne was able to watch the two men standing. Richard had one booted foot on the seat and William faced him, grim faced and serious.

'He has become far too bold!' William said thoughtfully.

'We both know what he is after too! He must not be allowed to get it either!' Richard said through gritted teeth. 'There is far too much at stake now!'

'There certainly is!' William agreed.

Anne frowned her bewilderment, completely lost with this mystifying conversation, which could have been in a second language.

'He'll be in a heavy disguise!' Richard commented thoughtfully, rubbing a chin that needed a shave.

William gave a heavy sigh. 'The trouble is he excels at that!'

Richard nodded, thinking deeply, a slight frown on his high forehead. This revelation was obviously something he had not quite expected, and certainly not so soon.

'This can only mean we are approaching the climax!' he murmured.

'Where is Bolingbroke, do you know?' was William's next question, which was equally baffling to Anne. These men's names meant nothing at all, yet they were obviously of crucial importance to Richard and William. Richard bit his lip, thinking deeply, while William stood with worry etched on his forehead.

Richard gave a small shrug and removed his feet from the seat. 'He has gone and we can both guess where and why!'

'That's true!' William agreed, and gritted his teeth, flashing them in the lantern's yellow glow. Richard fidgeted and Anne's heart rose in her mouth as, turning, he started a slow stride down the passage with William at his side, both of them talking animatedly, their steps slow and quiet. Anne strained but even her extra-sharp hearing could not pick out words; just the muted rumble of two masculine voices. They turned at the end and strolled back toward her. She held her breath. What had they been saying?

Once more they stopped automatically at the seat and Williams spoke first, his voice firm and positive.

'I don't like it!' he said flatly.

Richard gave a tiny shrug. 'Neither do I!' he replied coolly. 'But I can't think of anything

111

else, can you?'

William considered, gave a great sigh as repugnance flitted over his features, while he shook his head unhappily.

'That girl is stubborn, obstinate, opinionated and too highly spirited!' he said, his voice heavy with meaning.

'Oh!' Richard broke in. 'What's this? Have you two had a fight?' he asked with some amusement, showing the first lightening of mood.

'Fight?' William exclaimed. 'She was ready to run me through with a pitchfork!' and he carefully related what had happened, without any exaggeration or excuse.

Anne swallowed uneasily and pulled a moue. Richard started to chuckle as he stood with his hands on his hips. 'She did that?'

'It's no laughing matter, Master!' William replied coldly. 'She made me feel an absolute fool. Thank God, the boys don't know about it. I would lose all discipline with them! That girl is too bold for her own good. She's going to end up coming a cropper. She certainly doesn't know her station in life.'

'Which is?' Richard asked dryly.

William paused, wrong-footed by the question. He gave a loud sniff of disgust. Then his expression became a little more placid. 'I must say, though, you are right. She can ride and handle horses like a man!'

'I had forgotten that black mare. As you say,

the girl handles her well and I never go back on my word. A gift is a gift. Also, to be frank, William, you are a little bit inclined to over-bit the horses. You do that with a spirited creature like the black mare, and you are asking for trouble!'

William was deeply stung. 'If I do as you say, it is so that you will have instant control under all circumstances!' he replied huffily.

Richard stepped forward and slapped William on his back. 'I know! I know!' he soothed.

Slightly modified, William eyed him again. 'But that's not all either! She had a real set-to with Jenny, though it served Huggins right. She's been asking for it!'

'Jenny?' Richard groaned. 'I don't want her upset, I'll never find a cook as good as her again!'

'You want a bully who terrorises a young maid who cannot answer back?' William asked in a low voice.

Richard stiffened. 'All right! Tell me!'

William did, and Richard's expression became stern. He waited without comment until William finished, then shook his head.

'The girl was right!' he said slowly. 'I won't tolerate such behaviour. Katie is such a timid thing, she cannot weigh more than six stone wet through. I'll speak to Jenny!' he said sternly.

William shook his head vigorously. 'That

113

might not be politic, Master!'

'Why on earth not?'

William paused reflectively and Richard threw him a queer look, but said nothing as William continued. 'The girl has shown she can look after herself and if you go and speak to Jenny you might exacerbate the situation between the two females. And it takes a bold man to do that!' he said dryly.

Richard pulled a face. 'I take your point, but—?'

'Let Katie be with the girl all the time. That way Jenny has no authority over her, and I have a feeling she would think long and hard before she tried anything else,' he grinned.

'Yes, you're right as usual!'

Anne shook her head a little. This was the oddest relationship she had ever known. At times it was William who acted the master of Richard, who obeyed. It was unnatural, against anything she had ever known, and the unusual bothered Anne, if it failed to fit into the normal pattern of life. Could it be possible that William had some kind of hold upon Richard? He had shown he was forceful and ruthless; not one to be beholden to any other human being. A man without seeming sentiment, one whom Anne suspected could kill quite easily to save his life or thwart opposition—yet look how easily he deferred to William! She was utterly bewildered by this relationship, as well as what she had overheard, not one word of which had made sense, except when it referred to herself.

The two men strolled away again to the far end of the passage, talking fast. They stopped and appeared to have some kind of heated discussion and Anne writhed impotently. What could they be discussing so fervently? Was it herself once more? Their voices rumbled louder as they strolled back again.

'Well,' Richard said slowly, 'that has to be it, unless you can come up with something better?'

'No!'William admitted slowly. 'But that doesn't mean to say I like it one bit!'

'I'm not exactly clapping my heels myself!' Richard replied slowly.

'When?' was William's next blunt question.

'As soon as the situation clarifies itself. It might be next week or next month even!'

'But no longer!!'William added. 'No one dare wait longer!'

Richard yawned. 'God, I'm tired!' he said as his shoulders slumped. 'I'm off for my bed.You coming now?'

'Good idea!!'

Anne froze in panic.They could not just go like that, she thought wildly. She strained to hear, but their steps receded in unison. The stables' door clicked too, and she knew she was alone. She sat up, her mind churning with agitation, dissatisfied like a hungry man who has only been offered a crust when he expects a repast. Then an awful thought dawned.

She slipped hastily down the stairs with a thumping heart, while panic pounded. She ran from the stables' block, feet light and quick on the cobbled yard and reached the back door. She lifted the latch and pushed. The door had been bolted from the inside, and she was locked out.

Without thinking, she slipped into the shadows, where the house wall recessed. An owl whooshed overhead and made her flinch with shock as one hand flew to stifle a shriek. Her heart hammered frantically against her rib cage so she closed her eyes, and slowly counted to ten. She must think what to do.

Exactly where did Katie sleep? She knew it was on the attic row with Dan and Joel. It would never do to awaken the stable boys and where did Mary Bates sleep now that she had started to live in following Katie's new position?

The clouds drifted past, very slowly, with the moon flitting in and out erratically, now and again dancing down in a silver shaft. Anne gritted her teeth. She could not stand in the yard until dawn. But neither must anyone find her here either.

Somewhere on her right a small stone clinked against another and Anne froze, while her heart increase its tempo out of fright. Her ears twitched as another sound reached her. No animal could possibly make it and she wondered if she was visible, then commonsense told her this was impossible except from close-up.

She heard a light footstep with another sound, a slight whooshing as supple leather shoe soles moved on dry cobbles. She shrank back even further, frightened out of her wits, trembling as something deadly slid down her spine.

The shadow moved, openly coming into view as a male. Anne held her breath with fear as she gazed mesmerised at the man's face. His left hand rested on a sword hilt that hung on his right side, and he moved it away as if content he was alone. Anne guessed he was a rare left-handed swordsman. She prayed she would neither sneeze nor sniff as her terror increased without exactly knowing why. There was something quite feral about the man's smooth, soft steps, and she knew instinctively he was highly dangerous.

The intruder moved another step, then halted to study the area slowly and methodically. His head turned towards the stables and he scanned every inch of his surroundings. He took his time with a detailed examination, which included the house, looking up to the chimney pots, at the door and the windows.

Anne could see he was dressed in dark clothing, and his figure was tall and lean. His face was thin and hawk-like with a sharply pointed nose. She flinched inwardly as he moved a third time, and she was positive he must hear her pounding heart. Suddenly he looked directly at where she stood and Anne gazed back into dark pools of eyes, which burned hot with some savage fervour. She could see he was much older than herself or Richard, but younger than William. A sudden burst from the moon showed deep brown hair, without powder or wig, slightly thinning to one side. Was he some kind of law enforcer who suspected Richard's activities? If this was correct, she realised she could say nothing without giving herself away, which would never do. Anyhow, Richard seemed perfectly capable of taking care of himself and there was always William at his side. She shivered in the warm night air, then turning, saw the slightest suggestion of pink and grey in the east. Dawn would not be long, and she was still stuck in the yard. She must get back to the safety of her room, and with great relief she saw the left-handed swordsman softly pad away and disappear.

She made up our mind, bent and picked up a small piece of stone, then stepped from the comforting shadow. She eyed the upper windows and puckered her forehead. Surely that extreme one held a little jug with some flowers in it? It had to be Katie's!

With hope in her heart, she flung the gravel and waited. It tinkled against the glass pane with a noise of thunder to her. Holding her breath, biting her upper lip, she waited with heart racing again. At last, a little hand pulled one curtain aside, and a nose pressed against the glass.

Anne let out a sigh of relief and waved frantically. Katie caught the fluttering gesture, and her eyes were open wide with shock. Anne gesticulated at the door. For a few more seconds Katie stared, pop-eyed with astonishment, then her face vanished and Anne sighed, moving forward quietly to where she could wait. It seemed an age before she heard the two bolts slide back, and the door open carefully.

'Oh ma'am!' Katy gasped. 'You did not half give me a shock. I thought it was the devil itself, rattling my window!'

'Well, it's not the devil! It's just me!' Anne hissed back. 'And I want my room!'

'What have you been doing?' Katy whispered, as Anne stepped inside, and slid the bolts home once more.

'I could not sleep,' Anne lied quickly. 'I came out for a breath of fresh air and was locked out accidentally by someone coming in late.'

Katie accepted this easily. 'Probably the master coming home late!' she agreed.

Anne waited a moment, worried deeply as she stared at the maid. Katie's face held no questioning suspicion but she must be sure she did not talk. She took Katie's hand into her own.

'Let's keep this secret!' she implored and realised this would not do at all. 'He might not like to think I went out in the dark though I was perfectly safe. And I won't do it again. I'll just open my window wide when I want some fresh air!' she improvised hurriedly.

Katie considered this. She was far more shocked than Anne realised but, at the same time, she was a simple, naive person. Because she herself was quite unadventurous, it never entered her head she was listening to a pack of lies. She nodded, and threw Anne a gentle smile. The fact she so admired the other was another factor that halted any other interpretation.

'Cone on!' Anne whispered with agitation. 'We shall both be in awful trouble if the master—or Jenny—sees us here at this hour!' she pointed out.

'Quick!' Katie said, and giggled a little hysterically. Mistress Anne was fun to be with. She did such unusual things, but if Jenny did catch them—Katie's face turned white with terror.

They scampered back upstairs, with the maid in the lead and Anne sighed with relief as she reached her room. She clutched Katie's hand at the door for a moment.

'Thank you a thousand times!' she breathed. 'Our secret then? Promise?' She persisted.

Katie's heart swelled. If ever she had had a sister she would have loved one like Mistress Anne. As it was, the feelings she had for the other girl were so huge and warm she had no words to explain them. She nodded happily, bobbed a little curtsy, and sped back up the next flight to her own room.

Anne shut her door and half-collapsed on her bed as shock hit her. She closed her eyes, and immediately saw the man's face once more, flinching as she recalled his wicked mask with sharp nose and narrow, dark eyes. Then she went back over what she had overheard and frowned with bewilderment. None of it made sense, except that something of critical importance concerning the two men's activities was due to happen in the immediate future. She considered carefully and nodded her head sagely. Obviously someone, somewhere was going to be robbed by a highwayman, because it was known he would be carrying something of great value. Her lips tightened. Why did she feel a stab of disappointment to realise William too was so involved with Richard? As the older man, especially with the way he often talked to the master, surely he should be weaning Richard away from such illegal activities? Instead, he obviously encouraged them! If the night's intruder was connected with law enforcement surely she should warn them? She debated carefully, aware that such disclosure could only be bound up with her own conduct. A sharp shiver ran down her spine. She had seen Richard angry and knew she did not care to arouse him again into such a mood. She turned it all over in her mind, puzzled, pondered, and when dawn came properly, was no nearer a sensible solution.

With reluctance, she knew she had to keep her mouth shut. Perhaps one day, a situation might arise, which she could seize and turn to her advantage and in that manner only inform the men. Until then, while she lived in this shadowy house, discretion must be the watchword for her own safety, and that of Katie.

She sighed as she splashed cold water on her face. It helped to brighten a tired mind, but it was vital she went downstairs as if she had had an ordinary night's sleep. Jenny had sharp eyes, which missed nothing. After she had broken her fast she expected Richard to come to see her but, by eavesdropping, near the kitchen door, she learned he had already gone out. Was this connected with last night?

She rode out with Joe, not wanting to talk, concentrating solely upon her mare's pleasurable paces, yet she did not stay long. For some reason, she fidgeted to be back at the house, yet, when she did return she felt on edge still. Finally she took Katie and they went to walk together.

Katie had set ideas upon her position in life,

especially when out of doors with her wonderful mistress. Dutifully, she strolled one place behind Anne's back in the approved manner. Anne wore one of her new gowns because Katie had tactfully removed those left behind by the previous occupant. It was a light grey, trimmed with white lace and buttons. On her feet she wore shoes of kid, which fitted snugly and which whispered on the cobbled streets.

Anne wanted to talk, but Katie would lag behind so she stopped and turned. 'Walk level with me!'

Katie went scarlet and shook her head. 'I can't do that, ma'am. It's not fitting!'

Anne scowled. 'Fitting fiddlesticks!' she exclaimed with exasperation. 'I want company, and I can't talk to you behind me, can I?' she asked reasonably.

Katie had to accept this logic and, smiling, stepped forward one pace. Anne's eyes twinkled with pleasure and her heart warmed even more to this slip of a girl, who was so thin, yet only a little shorter than herself. At last they were able to chatter although Anne did most of this, bubbling to make sounds to keep back the worries buried in her heart.

The streets were crowded once they left their quiet area. They bustled with humanity and Anne wondered where everyone was going and why. The girls walked slowly, Anne's eyes swivelling in all directions. She stopped now and again to watch carriages pass with elegant ladies and gentlemen escorts. Every detail of attire was noted by her. She also studied the walkers and riders. She gazed at various homes, then at the vendors' stalls; nothing escaped her eyes and London became heady with strange, bustling excitement which, at the same time, was claustrophobic to a country-bred girl.

'Are the streets always as busy as this, Katie?' she wanted to know.

The maid nodded and pulled a face. 'Over there in that direction are very bad parts, where the quality dare not venture.'

It had dawned upon Katie that Mistress Anne was rather over bold. It was true, she was also very brave, but the maid realised that in London it was she who had the greater experience. She was also very conscious of her duty as attendant and chaperone.

'Do you know much of London?' Anne wanted to know next.

Katie shook her head firmly. 'Only around where we live,' she explained. A thought had been buzzing in her head for a while, and it made her cheeks glow pink. She lowered her eyes, suddenly uncertain.

'What is it?' Anne asked kindly.

Katie hesitated, highly embarrassed. She peeped at her mistress, then away again, her flesh turning to a brilliant red of shyness and uncertainty.

'Tell me!' Anne invited, both puzzled and amused. 'I don't mind!'

Katie perked up her courage. 'Are you the master's new mistress?' Then she halted. What on earth had come over her to ask such an awfully private question?

Anne almost hooted with laughter. She stopped. 'No, I am not!' she said with quiet firmness.

'Oh!' Katie said, then tilted her head to one side. 'Are you his lady then? I mean, are you going to wed him?!'

'No!' Anne replied flatly.

'Oh!' Katie exclaimed again, as her expression became sad. 'Does that mean you will go away soon?'

Anne now understood the drift of the conversation, and she was touched to recognise the disappointment in Katie's voice. She felt humble to know that she was liked for what she was yet she had no idea how to reply.

Katie took a deep breath, then burst forth in a gamble of courage. 'When you go, ma'am, can I please come with you?' she asked hopefully. 'I'd dress your hair for you and look after your clothes, and you're not have to pay me anything at all just as long as I could be with you, because I'd only want a bit of food and a corner to sleep in, and I would—!'

'Katie! Katie!' Anne said softly, taking the maid's hand. She saw tears of worry in her eyes and her heart went out to her. There was a sharp pinched look on Katie's face and her mouth corner was puckered with distress. 'But Katie, I am only—!' Anne halted uncertainly. What exactly was she indeed? Richard's companion? That rang false to start with, because she had hardly seen him since she entered his house. His woman? Never! His servant? No! She was a superfluous, useless nonentity, with neither place nor purpose, so *why* exactly had he wanted her to come with him?

'Katie, I have no idea how long I will be in London,' she replied with as much smoothness as her troubled thoughts could muster. 'One day I will certainly go away, but when—I have no idea. What I will promise you is this. When I do go, you can come with me if you like!'

It was a reckless statement. She knew this as soon as the words had popped out and for a second panic gripped her.Where would she go? What could she do? On what could the two of them live? She watched delight flash in Katie's eyes and Anne was forced to avert her gaze with acute embarrassment. She would keep her promise, she vowed and deal with the awesome problems as they arose. She squeezed the maid's hand encouragingly.

'Come on, let's continue our walk!' But as she turned, her eyes opened wide with shock. She caught her breath, while her grip tightened on Katie's arm.

'What is it, ma'am?' Katie asked

bewildered. Anne had changed before her eyes and gone all tense.

'Quick!' Anne whispered. 'Walk this way!' she said, and grabbed Katie's arm to pull her aside. 'I want to watch that man over there.The one in dark brown breeches and coat, who wears his sword on the right-hand side!'

Anne increased her speed and Katie was forced to scurry to keep up. People regarded the two girls a little curiously, but Anne was oblivious, intent only on keeping him in sight.

'We are being unladylike!' Katie protested and Anne slowed her pace. It would be stupid to draw attention to themselves. 'Who is he, ma'am?'

'That's what I'd like to know!' Anne muttered but more to herself. 'Have you ever seen him before?'

Katie shook her head. The man's clothes were well cut, and of excellent material. He strode with confidence. His dress was so fine he might have been labelled a fop, except there was something about his gliding walk that reminded Katie of a hunting cat.

The man stopped and looked up at a building. Anne turned and stared into a window that displayed ribbons and lace. She studied the man's reflection. Now he had turned—was he looking at her? Her heart started to thud uneasily. She studied the lean figure with a sharp nose and judged his age to be in the early thirties.

Two carriages passed, which broke off her view. The horses' hooves raised a small cloud of dust. Some riders came in the opposite direction; two talking couples passed them, then a few young girls, escorted by two stern-faced matrons.

'Katie, come on! We can't just stand here, let's go back to the house!' Anne said, feeling acute alarm without quite knowing why. Surely nothing could happen in these crowded streets yet she was filled with unease.

The man moved suddenly, crossed the road, dodged between horses and headed straight for them. Anne forced a nonchalant expression, though a pulse throbbed in her neck and she felt sweat dapple her forehead. She made herself stand quietly with the maid as if they expected someone. Katie went to speak, saw her mistress was tense and changed her mind.

The strange man approached, drew level with them and looked right into Anne's eyes with an unblinking, enigmatical gaze. Anne knew then! Her instinct flared a violent warning. He had seen her in the yard and done nothing. Why? Was she now some kind of target, and if so, for what purpose? Surely, he did not think she was connected with a highwayman's activities? Something cold chased down her spine, and she gave a little shiver.

'Did he nod to you?' Katie whispered.

'I hope not!' Anne replied with considerable feeling. She gave herself a brisk shake. 'Come on, I'm daydreaming!' she told Katie quickly. 'Let's go home and perhaps you'll help me wash my hair.'

Katie was glad to move again. The strange man had cast an uneasy gloom upon her mistress and she had no idea why.

Anne did not walk again for two days. She had brief morning rides, then spent the remainder of the time reading. Her desire to learn was enormous, and plenty of reading material was available for her. At the same time, her mind was constantly filled with the events and her surreptitious knowledge. She attacked her thoughts from many directions, but kept coming back to the only possible answer. The frightening man had to have some kind of connection with Richard's highway activities.

She was pleased to discover that William was not quite as hostile. It was true he could not be called friendly, but Anne sensed the distance he exhibited was more a result of occupied mind than distaste for her presence. Even Jenny had cooled down. Not that Anne trusted her one iota, but her enmity was muted, and she even managed to be polite so obviously someone had spoken to her.

Once or twice, she thought of the farm with absolute amazement. It was only a few short weeks ago, but it seemed like a lifetime. Was it possible she had laboured so hard? She studied her hands. No longer were they ugly. The hideous calluses had been removed and the skin softened. Anne grinned at them. If she tried hard labour now, they would blister in no time. She was getting to look too much like a lady of the quality and that was nonsense. Try as she might, learn what she could, she was realistic enough to remember she was a bastard, who did not even know her mother, let alone a pedigree. Then her natural resilience would rise. She was Anne Howard, for better or worse even if there was no natural niche for a hybrid like herself.

EIGHT

Anne's frustration reached an irritating pitch, and she felt downright miserable as well as keyed up to an unbearable pitch.

On this particular sunny day, she felt stifled. With all the houses around, and the crowded streets, she knew exactly how the butterfly felt when caught in the net. She must get out, have some fresh air, and be alone for a little while. Much as she liked the maid's company, Anne knew the claustrophobic feeling would not abate unless she were by herself.

William had been away for most of the

morning, and Dan explained he wasn't due back until later. Anne made up her mind, and, turning back, pulled off one of the good gowns and slipped on that which she kept solely for riding. It was soiled at the edges, where the mare sweated but it had a good familiar aroma to her.

She padded downstairs and saw Katie doing some of her laundry, while Jenny laboured, making the most delectable smells come from her oven. The housekeeper's recent affability made Anne pause.

'That does smell good!' she complimented and Jenny lifted her head to throw her a thoughtful look. She was cautious now with the master's guest since he had spoken forcefully to her. Initially, she considered Mistress Anne had told tales, but, later on, learned it was William. Very gradually it had begun to enter Jenny's head that perhaps there was more to this young girl than met the eye. Certainly, she never trespassed in the kitchen. She was very polite and praised her cooking lavishly without being too fulsome. Jenny had begun to lose a little of her natural antagonism as the days passed. Mistress Anne was no longer a stranger; simply an unusual woman. The maid's transfer still rankled a little, but deep in Jenny's mind was a frustrating problem that kept her mental processes fully occupied.

'I'm going out!' Anne announced. 'I want some fresh air!' she finished blithely.

Alarm crossed Jenny's face, and Katie displayed concern. Both knew that Dan had slipped out to see the fodder merchant with an order, which only left Joe on the premises. Neither Jenny nor Katie had much faith in Joe, who had too big an opinion of himself for their liking. For once, maid and housekeeper were united.

'William is still out!' Jenny commented uneasily for Mistress Anne's face wore a stubborn look. 'Only Joe is here'

'I don't need him!' she said lightly and walked over to the stables. Jenny hurried after her, thoroughly alarmed, and the maid pattered at her heel rather like a terrier puppy following a huge bulldog.

'You mustn't go alone!' Jenny cried at Anne's retreating back.

Anne misinterpreted the statement. Quite suddenly, it sounded as if Jenny were dictating to her again. Her hackles rose: 'Why not?' she demanded truculently.

'Because it is not done,' Jenny replied, then moved onto more sure ground. 'And because the Master said you are not to!'

Anne knew this was perfectly correct, but boredom, the fidgets and mischief combined into one ball. 'I'll not ride in town, so what does it matter?'

Jenny caught sight of the young groom. 'Joe!' she barked. 'Mistress Anne is going riding. You are to escort her!' she ordered abruptly.

Anne scowled with fury, opened her mouth to argue, then snapped it shut. Joe would follow at a discreet distance, and she knew her mare's speed outdistanced that of any horse here, except those ridden by Richard. The mischief changed to pure devilment.

She flashed a sweet smile at Joe. 'Will you, Joe?'

Jenny turned around at this sudden capitulation and looked with worry at Katie. 'She is up to something!' she said in a low voice.

'I'm afraid so. But what can we do?' Katie asked with concern.

Joe was secretly delighted. Riding was always more interesting than stable work, and it was usually Dan who enjoyed that pleasure. Jenny bit her lip. This meant the establishment would be without a male protector until Dan returned, which would never do. She turned the Katie.

'I don't like it. Look! You go and see if you can find Dan and bring him straight back. Do you know where the fodder merchants are situated?'

'I think so, and I'll be quick!' Katy promised, turned and trotted into the house to put on outdoor shoes. She too was alarmed and felt glad to be able to do something positive to help wonderful Anne. If only she were not quite so headstrong and brave.

133

Anne saddled her mare herself. All of the blues had vanished in a twinkling, and she was out in the yard mounted by the time Joe led his horse out.

'Ride at my rear, Joe!' and she grinned down at Jenny. 'Don't fret! I'll be fine!'

Anne walked her mare from the yard and turned in the direction she knew led to countryside. Night was fresh and on her toes, bouncing along, grinding the snaffle bit, anxious to stretch her long legs in a gallop.

Anne was used to being stared at by other people, as she rode on the man's cross saddle and not at all disconcerted. Let people be shocked. Some of these stuffy Londoners could do with waking up, she thought as she peeped behind. Joe rode three horse lengths at her rear and a grin was set on Anne's face. She meant it when she said she wished to be alone. She would bide her time, then a situation would be bound to arise when Joe's slower horse would be left standing.

They moved away quickly from the crowds on to a well-used road while ahead stretched a thin straggle of cottages, then open land. The black mare arched her neck and started to pull but Anne's hands were firm on the reins. A coach came towards them, pulled by four sweating greys. The horn sounded its warning blast, demanding priority passage and Anne heeled Night aside. She glanced back and saw her opportunity. Joe also was forced to pull well over, because the road here was narrow, with slightly sloping banks. As the coach drew level, Joe's horse bucked an angry protest at the noise and, for a few seconds, he was heavily engaged in retaining his seat.

Anne saw people inside the coach staring with amused interest. Another distant observer was a rider on a liver chestnut, which had an outstanding white blaze. The man ignored Joe, but looked over at Anne.

She sniffed to herself. Another male who disapproved of females riding astride. Then the mischief devil exploded. She touched with her heels and released her reins. Night did not require a second invitation. She was fit and fresh; she flung herself into a wild gallop.

Anne laughed with glee.This was real fun! The air whistled around her cheeks, tousling her hair and she was free. Free at last!

'Faster!' she cried wildly and touched with her heels again.

Night was surprised, but obliged. The mare unleashed herself into a speed that astonished Anne, and nearly caught her unawares. She flung her body weight forward and swiftly readjusted her balance. She stood in her stirrup irons, weight over the mare's sliding shoulders, while her knees slammed tight on the saddle flaps. Her heels were low, to give maximum grip from thigh to groin and Night could gallop, completely unhindered by her rider's body weight.

'Come on, my beauty! Let's leave them all behind!' Anne hissed urgently.

She thought her mare was at top speed but one black ear twitched with acknowledgement and the mare unleashed herself once more. Her black hooves sped over the ground in a rattling tattoo.The black nose poked forward as her neck stretched, while her tail flowed a horizontal flag.

Anne screamed with wonder. She had never ridden so fast before nor dreamed Night had such incredible speed packed into her compact frame. Her power was exhilarating; her pace hypnotic.

On some stretches of land cattle grazed quietly from nearby villages, yet of human life she saw no one. She tightened her reins and pulled the mare back and Night came willingly to the bit now that the first flush of enthusiasm had waned.

Anne let out her breath, watching white sweat coat the black neck. She stretched herself and looked casually to her rear. She had totally lost Joe but who was that coming up purposefully in her rear? It was a liver chestnut with a white blaze, and she had a flashing memory of the male rider, staring at her just before she rode off.

A cold warning prickled the nape of her neck so she frowned and looked around uneasily. Why did her blood chill? The chestnut horse lacked Night's speed and would be more blown than the mare who had rested and recovered from her mad dash. Anne sat in the saddle and stared hard, trying to make out detail.

She caught her breath. The rider was still too far away to pick out facial details, but there was no mistaking a sword hilt worn on the opposite side of the body. A wave of fear caught at the back of her throat as instinct told her it was the eerie, midnight prowler. His appearance here was no coincidence. Was that a pistol he carried? She could not be sure.

Why should such a heavily armed man pursue her? It must be, it had to be, her connection with Richard. Did he think he could make her tell him whatever he wanted to know? Her obstinacy rose as she scowled.

She shortened her reins and gave a gentle nudge with her heels. Now was neither the time nor the place to attempt to conduct an investigation into the mystery. She was far too alone, and wished now Joe was with her. Perhaps she had been foolishly precipitate with her actions and she gulped.

Night had fully recovered her wind and was keen to gallop again, but Anne kept her to a steady canter. She had no idea how long she would need the mare's strength, nor how she was going to dodge the man to get back to the city.

She kept throwing estimating glances backwards and saw the chestnut was strained.

Although he was a big, raw-boned horse he was neither as fit nor as well bred as the black mare. He carried a much heavier load on his back, which the man did not distribute as easily as he might have. He was not a clumsy rider, but he lacked the natural ability to flow with his mount.

Anne was not worried, though she was annoyed at the disruption to their lovely free ride. They were heading farther out from the city, and she suspected if she should be late back there might well be some kind of panic. If Joe returned alone, which was more than likely and related he had lost her, Jenny and Katie would go into a high state of alarm. She remembered Richard's warnings not to be alone, and now guilt attacked her in little spurts.

The ground ahead was not as smooth. It was poached from where wandering cattle had sunk into the earth in the wet months so she rode warily. It would never do for the mare to come down and leave her unhorsed before this rider. She looked back again and saw how his chestnut had its ears back, with nostrils distended for maximum effort. The horse laboured badly.

She looked ahead and grinned and maliciously turned her mare in the direction of a large expanse of ploughed land that had been left to lie fallow that year. Night had no trouble picking her way daintily between the ridge and furrow at a controlled trot. When Anne looked behind once, she felt sorry for the other horse. Its large hooves slipped and slithered and it nearly came down, to make the man lurch in his saddle.

She wondered about the time or what to do next. It was foolish to keep going farther away. She made a swift decision, turned and rode back towards the rider. Now she could easily make out his sharp facial features, with narrow brown eyes, which bored into hers, expressionless, but calculating.

He stopped his horse, which hung his head and blew with distress, accompanied by heaving ribs. Night walked now, her hooves delicately spanning the range and furrow because Anne was suddenly wary.

She had no idea how far a pistol ball could carry so she kept a prudent distance away. The man sat still, and as she passed him at a distance, Anne wondered whether it was admiration that briefly flared in his eyes. She sat proud and direct, and her mare never put a hoof wrong. She appeared to glide over the earth.

'What do you want?' Anne shouted at him.

He did not reply, though his lips set, thin, tight and cruel. 'Leave me alone. Stop following me about! I have more than one protector!'

His silence aggravated as well as frightened. Anne halted Night a good distance away and studied him. He was well dressed in dark coat and breeches. She studied his weapons next. She knew nothing about them, but was sufficiently aware that he wore them with the same comforting familiarity as Richard. She guessed this meant he was good with both of them. There was nothing flamboyant or artificial about him.

'Who are you then?' was her next frustrated call.

The rider simply watched her, turning his head as she circled, his eyes calculating, narrow, with an expressionless face. She saw the fingers of his left hand flutter a little and alarm screamed a warning. With youth's speed, she neck-reined the mare aside and shot off at a tangent, only pulling up after a gallop of a short distance.

When she turned to face him she saw she had been wise. He had pushed his mount into a sharp little gallop, and the pistol was on his left hand. He pulled up then, aware he was quite out of range, and that she was better mounted. He had no chance of getting near to use any weapon and was wise enough not to try.

Anne fumed. She wanted to go back to London. Quite suddenly, the house that she had fretted to leave welcomed with its solid safety. How foolish she had been with her behaviour. Richard would be livid when he learned and this knowledge made her blanch guiltily. Richard Mason in a violent rage would be terrifying, and her guilt made her realise she could expect no ally from Katie, Jenny or William. Joe too might even hate her, if William had returned and hit him for letting her go free. She quailed inwardly, but no, she had to return. After all, she had promised Katie.

For the rest of them she cared nothing. She was of no consequence to them, so they were not her concern, yet how her heart swelled at this lie. She did have some regard for bad-tempered William. She liked quiet Mary. Even temperamental Jenny had become a living, breathing personality, while Richard Mason? With him her emotions were hopelessly confused, and she could not understand herself at all. She did not love him; such an idea was preposterous but her heart see-sawed violently. His good opinion was something she felt she would cherish. On those rare occasions when she saw him, he exhibited a gentle tenderness, which was at hopeless odds with the other side of his character. He was a complicated enigma to which she knew she was both repelled and attracted. Katie loved her. Of that she was quite positive, and her emotion for the maid bordered on that of a big sister for a younger one. Katie looked up to her, worshipped her, Katie wanted to be with her always. In Katie's eyes, she would never be able to do a great wrong. Katie's simple faith was the treasure of her heart—the one great gift she had been given since she left the farm. For this, it had all been worthwhile, and for Katie she would return and face Richard's undoubted wrath. If only this obnoxious man would go away.

She became aware of the sun sliding down to the west and calculated the time with a sinking heart. There would be panic at the house by now. Thank God, Richard was away. She could only pray she could be back before William returned as well. She would have to make some kind of peace with Joe, but she suspected he was amenable to feminine flattery.

She reached a decision, spun Night, around, rammed with her heels enough to make the mare grunt with shock and, down a straight line of plough, she shot her mount into a hard gallop. The man was taken aback, such a move was not one that he had anticipated.

Both girl and mare shot past in a black blur. He aimed his pistol, but the chestnut horse fidgeted, affected by the passing mare's speed. He bellowed something in a deep bass voice that Anne did not catch.

Then she was past and heading back towards the capital. She gave Night her head, consumed with anxiety, conscious of the rapidly passing time. She let the mare gallop for a long way then, peering behind and, realising the man had given up whatever he had planned, she pulled Night back into a walk to cool off. White sweat foamed the mare's neck and flanks and dropped from her bit while Anne too was sweaty from exertion and latent fear. Should she tell Richard now? How could she without giving herself away? She had a shrewd idea he would not take kindly to eavesdropping, and neither would William. She had a feeling the master and William had some trust for her, which they would certainly lose if they learned about her duplicity. No! It was better to keep her mouth shut for the time being. Whoever the man was, he could cause no disturbance at the house—surely?

It was nearly dusk when the mare walked into the stable yard, which was ablaze with light. Anne swung wearily from the saddle, then flinched as she saw William. He spotted her, his face set grim.

'Master! She's back!' he roared.

'What!' Richard cried and emerged from the stable block.

Anne stood with a sinking heart. This she had not anticipated at all and she saw a thundercloud descend on Richard's face.

Richard Mason had been thankful to get home after an exhausting period away. To learn Anne had vanished, leaving a woebegone Joe, had made him erupt. William had only returned minutes beforehand, and both men had stormed after exchanging worried looks. Joe had protested vehemently, frightened for his skin, then William had sent him flying with a hammer blow.

'You useless fool!' William had snarled. 'Letting a girl still wet behind the ears pull a fast one on you. I've a good mind to throw you out without a reference, so you can beg on the streets!'

Richard had been appalled. A country girl had no idea, despite all he had said, of the dangers in the current life. What really infuriated him, though, was the fact she had disobeyed him. And this at a time when there was so much at stake. The fact she had no knowledge cut no ice with him. Death was a daily, even hourly, companion to him. To have a crisis like this, upon his return, one which was totally unnecessary, was the final straw. He flashed a look at William compounded from barely controlled rage, mental and physical exhaustion, downright fright at their position and something else. If anyone had hurt Anne Howard—and his mind refused to react any more for a moment.

He strode over to her, grabbed one arm with fingers of steel and glowered at her. 'To your room!' he snarled.

And was shocked at the mask on his face and obeyed without thinking, leaving her mare standing, head lowered, tired and wanting her oats. She hurried indoors and stumbled on the stairs, with Richard one pace behind. Tactfully, Katie and Jenny placed themselves in the kitchen behind a shut door.

He opened the door to her room, shoved her inside, slammed it, then stood white-faced with anger. 'You stupid bitch!' he hissed at her. 'As if I haven't enough on—!' He paused and took a deep breath. 'Where the hell have you been? What do you think you are doing, losing the stable boy on purpose? William is right! It's time someone sorted you out!' he shouted at her, releasing some of his tension.

Anne struggled to collect her scattered wits. She had known he would be cross, but had never envisaged this fearsome, deadly cold rage. Anyone would think she had committed a murder. His eyes held a cruel, cold glare from which sparks appeared to sheet. His lips were two thin bands of dark red while his neck muscles stood out in stark relief.

'I told you never to ride alone and when I give orders they are obeyed!' he bellowed at her.

'Don't roar at me like that!' she shouted back, feeling tears of guilt prickle. She knew she had done wrong, but this outward show of superior masculine strength did not prod her conscience at all. It merely amused her own natural antagonism. Her face turned scarlet with humiliation and resentment and she tossed her head, making her hair fly as if in a wind.

This defiant gesture was too much for him. He leapt forward, grabbed both her shoulders, and shook her furiously. His large hands were iron clamps, and his powerful arms flung her body to left and right as if it had been made of rags. Anne was sure afterwards her teeth rattled. Then she lost her own temper at his mauling. She kicked out at his shins, but missed, so she tried to claw his hands free, which was futile. She found herself breathing in great, gasping sobs, when suddenly he released one hand and cracked it down hard on her cheek.

She went flying across the bed. Her mind was bemused, temporarily, and he leapt after her without thought or reason. She lay stunned for a few seconds, with the shock of his power and resisted automatically. They grappled wildly. She spat and tried to bite, as she twisted and writhed, then her teeth latched on one forearm. She sank them in savagely.

He let out a yowl of pain, turned to free his arm and she bit him again. He hit her, a savage backhander with considerable force behind it. Anne's head spun, so she brought up her knee and tried to emasculate him with a savage kick. He saw it at the last moment, and turned wildly.

One of his hands gripped her bodice and the stitching parted in a violent rip, then he struggled to hold both of her wrists. Now they fought in silent rage, each wholly intent upon the other's destruction. She managed to grab a handful of ruffled shirt, which tore. He snatched at her skirt and those seams parted in a giant tear.

Anne twisted, writhed, bit and clawed.

He ducked, dodged, squirmed and pressed with his strong hands.

Anne was powerful for a female, and Richard was hard put to hold her still. He knew he should use a fist and knock her out but his hot rage had gone, to be replaced with the colder, more deadly variety.

They rolled off the bed and crashed on the floor, broke apart, sprang to their feet and immediately leapt at each other. Anne raged silently, but breathed heavily. He swore once, then concentrated on trying to hold her still, amazed at her strength.

Another section tore from her gown. Two more rips appeared in his shirt, and now they wrestled silently, except for grunts and sobs, half-naked and oblivious to this.

Anne was awed by whipcord muscles and his bottomless strength. Gradually, he had started to dominate her, though his chest heaved and he streamed with sweat. They crashed back on the bed, which groaned in a protest, fighting like alley cats without any noise though. Anne was underneath now, and he gripped her wrists, pinning her body with one pointed knee.

'Hell cat!' he swore at her.

'Swine!' she spat back at him.

For a few seconds, they paused. Each

laboured to breath while sweat cascaded down their faces. He was stark naked from the waist up, and displayed pectoral muscles and a skin with only the lightest covering of golden hair. His biceps were of the long thin kind, filled with power. His neck was enormous, muscles and sinew etched against his skin but it was also dappled with blood from her nails. The drawstring of his breeches had become loose and very gradually they had worked their way down.

Anne was in a similar condition. There was very little left of the top of her gown, certainly nothing strategic was hidden. Her naked breasts, heaving wildly, swelled up at him, each full, rose-tipped and inviting. She breathed heavily, half sobbing with the effort, conscious her skirt had also parted, and she lay with her remaining small clothes indecently shredded.

Their eyes met and held. Very slowly, the battle light faded, as they began to study each other as male and female. Her lips opened a little, and he watched with fascination as her tongue darted nervously near her fine, white teeth.

Slowly, still a little uncertain and untrusting, he lowered his head and their lips met, touched and pressed. For just a few seconds Anne's temper continued to storm, then it sizzled out. His body was quite magnificent. It held perfection in the way muscles and tendons moved smoothly with grace and beauty. There was something alluring and tempting about him.

He moved on his side, swiftly divested himself of his breeches and small clothes, while she ripped away the gown's remnants. Slowly, and little warily now, she opened her legs invitingly. As he came down to enter her, she arched willingly, her hands playing with the muscles of his back, then he began to move joyfully. This time they were free with each other, savouring, exploring, falling in with each other's tempo, united satisfactorily, their tempo mutual and rising. They built up gradually to a peak, with him leading the way, anxious to prolong himself so she could enjoy maximum satisfaction. As she began to mew like a kitten, he felt fresh waves of himself surge along, lifting her with him. Their climax was an explosion, which left them both smiling tenderly, supremely happy.

He slid from her and turned so they lay side by side, arms around each other, her head on his chest while he nuzzled her hair. He stroked her, wanting to give all the love and security that was in him. He wanted to keep her eyes hidden while he examined himself with retrospective awe. His mind revolved with discovery and wonder. Of all the females he had taken, and there had been plenty, there was not one capable of touching the well spring of his heart. Long ago, he had resigned himself to the fact no female could. Yet this wild, brave, crazy girl had shown herself capable of unleashing the tremendous depth of sensitivity and feeling that he had not known he possessed.

Anne heard the powerful beat of his heart and breathed in his sweat as she clung to him, blissfully at peace for the very first time in her life. In her naïveté, she had often wondered what she might feel when taken to the height of true physical ardour. Her mind continued to reel with the wonder of it all, the ultimate bliss when two bodies fuse into one. The possibility of a new pregnancy worry never entered her head.

'That was better, wasn't it?' he whispered.

Anne reached up and stroked his cheek. 'It was wonderful!' she murmured.

He gave a sigh of replete happiness, and allowed himself another minute of undiluted joy with her, then gradually, awareness replaced this. The warmth went from his eyes as he gave a tiny shake to his head.

'I nearly went out of my mind when I returned and found you missing!' he told her sincerely. 'Don't ever frighten me like that again!'

'I was quite all right,' she replied softly. 'I'm sorry I caused such alarm. Nothing happened to me, you can see!' she paused. 'I did so enjoy my ride. You should see Night go!'

She could tell him nothing now. The crazy left-handed swordsman must be peculiar, not

150

quite sane. Neither could she tell him one word that would lead to the revelation of her eavesdropping. Nothing must mar their present quite perfect symmetry.

'You have been luckier than you realise, when I think of some of the bad men around,' he told her gently. 'You stay around the house now though. You have Katie for company, and, I suspect, she worships the ground on which you walk. And I forbid you to ride again when both myself and William are absent!' he pointed out, with quiet firmness.

A tiny frown crinkled her forehead. She must make him understand. She would not be a prisoner here. She must be able to get out and about to where there was grass and freshness. The London streets were stiflingly uncomfortable for any length of time.

'Katie is good company,' she agreed gently, 'but there's a limit to where we can walk. Don't forget, Richard, I am a country girl, used to the fresh air and open spaces'

'That's true!' he agreed, but he knew he could not back down one inch now. 'You must do as I say, though. In this matter I must be obeyed!'

Anne, bit her lip. 'I can't!' she told him honestly. 'I'd explode, and hate it all here! Don't you see, Richard?'

He did not and would not. One girl's feelings were completely unimportant when there was so much at stake. The fact she knew nothing at all was irrelevant. He was the master, his orders must be obeyed, because upon him rested so much. He looked into her face and studied it gravely with a sinking heart. It had started to wear a look of obstinacy.

'You have to obey me, Anne!' he told her even more firmly.

Anne pulled right away from him and sat up. How typically arrogant and masculine, she thought. He gives an order just because it suits him. All right, she had acted wrongly, and she would not be so stupid again but neither would she be imprisoned. She noted how his eyes had narrowed in a calculating manner.

'I'm not your prisoner!' she pointed out sharply.

'You'll damned well do as I say!' he barked.

'I won't!' she snapped back, her temper rising.

'You will!' he grated.

They scrambled off the bed, their passion completely forgotten. They faced each other again as naked protagonists.

'I am master here!' Richard said, just a little too pompously. His heart had sunk. She was becoming awkward once more, and he would not have it.

'I'm not your slave!' Anne flew back at him, feeling miserable inside, but determined not to yield just because he was stronger than her.

'You can't make me!' she ended with a snap.

'No?' he asked and his voice now held a

152

dangerous ring.

'No!' she shouted back, with rising temper.

' I can keep you locked in this room with a chamber pot for company!' he roared.

Anne's breasts heaved with passion. 'Then I'll scream and scream and scream so the whole of London hears me!' she promised, and meant it.

Richard half lifted his right hand. He did not intend a blow, more a light disciplinary tap but Anne misconstrued his gesture. She ducked and kicked as hard as she could. Her heel landed on his shinbone and he let out a short howl of pain and hopped wildly. She seized the chance and kicked the other leg in the same place.

'You bitch!' he spat at her.

Anne whipped around, darted forward, opened the door, and with one swift hand movement, had the presence of mind to grab a long robe to cover her nudity. She flung this around her body as she ran down the passage, slipping her arms in the sleeves, hastily tying the belt. She heard him calling and stumbling and guessed he was struggling to don his breeches and shredded shirt. Serve him right, she thought, but what next?

She scrambled down the stairs and, hearing a thud, guessed he had tripped. Instinctively, she fled to the stables, praying no one would be there. She had a fleeting, crazy idea, of untying Night, leaping on her back and riding wildly to freedom for ever.

She shot into the stables and one quick glance showed them empty. The horses lifted their heads at her sudden appearance, and she immediately slowed. She heard his steps and shivered with panic, then she spotted the pitchfork stuck in a bale of straw. What had worked once must surely do a second time. She grabbed it and backed against a wall.

Richard appeared, his ripped shirt looking worse than if he had been half naked. He had pulled on his breeches, but the drawstrings dangled loose. He halted and studied her, then casually tightened the strings in a slow, elaborate bow, taking time to tuck the ends away neatly, while he thought rapidly. He remembered William's recent predicament. His mind raced back to their recent lovemaking. He eyed the wild glare in her eyes and the steady way in which she held the fork and he knew he only had one course of action.

'Put that down!' he said, clearly and slowly as if talking to a small child.

'Make me!' she challenged hotly and waited. What could he do? The whip was in her hand not his but a tiny voice prodded at her heart. How could she sink such a lethal weapon in him?

Richard spoke in the same measured tone. 'I will tell you once more, and only once more. Put down that fork!'

Anne hesitated, uncertainly. She had

expected a tirade of anger from him not this calm, almost social conversational tone. Was she making some kind of error? What could he do? Wasn't he though just a little too self-confident? She bit her lip indecisively with trembling nerves, and watched him carefully.

He waited only a few seconds, his features impassive, then with a tiny almost sad shake off his head, turned and walked briskly into the saddle area. Anne heard him moving around as if looking for something and she waited with growing unease. She had a sick feeling he had some unknown trick to play on her to turn the tables. Rack her brains as she might, she could not think what this might be.

He walked slowly back one hand hidden. He strode past her and went to the black mare. Night turned her head, took in his scent with a flair of her nostrils and uttered a soft, inquiring nicker.

Richard faced her, looking back six paces and brought his arm forward, which held a pistol. It was long, black and ugly.

'This weapon is loaded, primed and ready to fire,' he told her evenly. 'I do not lie. I do not have to and I never bluff when I have a weapon in my hand. If you do not put down that fork and behave yourself by the count of ten, I shall put the ball through this mare's head,' he told her in a low voice.

Anne opened her mouth with horror as his cold-blooded words sank in. She froze with anguish and stared hard at him. His face was implacable, a mask deadlier than any she had ever seen before on a human being. He stood as if carved from stone, though a nerve thronged on the side of his neck. His eyes resembled those of an adder before it struck at a field mouse. He lifted the pistol slowly and raised it to within four inches of the mare's inquiring face.

'One!' he said carefully.

'No!' Anne shrieked. 'Not Night! She's mine! You gave her to me! You can't hurt her! She's done nothing!'

'Three! Four!' he droned evenly.

Anne jumped forward, and half lowered the fork to stare at him horrified. How utterly loathsome he was! What a blind fool, she had been.

'What kind of a monster are you to take your spite out of a dumb animal?' she screamed.

'Six!'

'Please don't hurt her!' she wailed hysterically.

'Seven!'

'Please?' and now she started to cry.

'Eight!'

'Oh! Damn your eyes!' she raged and flung the fork down. It landed with a clatter on the passage, startling the highly bred horses, making them toss their heads high with agitation. 'I hate you!' she stormed as tears flooded her cheeks. 'I think you are the most odious creature born. You will never, never, NEVER touch me again, you beast of a man!'

Anne shivered with shock, her shoulders shuddering as she cried freely. She felt as if someone had walked over her grave. She leaned against the wall and broke into a paroxysm of violent sobbing, crying as she had not since a small child. It took time for the bitter emotion to wash through her system but finally her tears ceased. She dried her eyes on a corner of the cloak, her face now snow white, but she made herself lift her head, turn and, with all the dignity she could muster, she walked from the stables, back to the house and the sanctuary of her room.

Richard felt his tension slowly wind down as he lowered the pistol and put it on safe. He closed his eyes as weariness flooded him. Her hatred had been a knife in the centre of his heart and he knew something in him had died. His expression was bleak when he opened his eyes. There was a discreet cough behind him from the end stall, and he whipped around, alert once more.

William appeared and looked over quizzically.

'I didn't know you were around,' Richard said slowly.

William shrugged. 'I was bending down, checking this horse's shoes when she burst in. And I was going to speak, then you came after her, and I thought discretion was the better part of valour. I bent down and stayed hidden,' he explained simply.

Richard gave a heavy sigh, and looked thoughtfully at the pistol barrel, rubbing a fingermark off almost absentmindedly. Finally he looked over at the old man, his eyebrows up in a silent question.

William understood. A grim smile touched his mouth corners. 'You did right!' he commented shortly.

'She will really hate me now just when I thought she was starting to like me,' Richard told him slowly.

William stepped up to the younger man and faced him squarely. 'Your likes, dislikes and emotional worries are of no consequence,' he replied sternly. After a pause he continued, 'And one headstrong girl is of no concern.'

Richard looked back at him frankly. 'We had just made love,' he said simply, as if that explained everything. 'I think she is—!' and he had to stop, his voice threatening to break.

William slapped him on the back, then spoke gruffly. 'No matter what you think, Anne Howard is—nothing in the grand scheme of things,' he said coldly. 'Remember yourself!'

Richard took another deep breath and nodded slowly before he looked into William's stern gaze. 'Why me?' he asked a little plaintively.

William had no immediate answer available. 'Many people in the past have asked that. I hope I don't have to knock backbone into you!' he said bluntly.

Richard forced a weak grin on his face. 'No!' he replied quickly. 'I'm all right now, but I think I'll keep out of her way for a bit. Thank God I'm away soon. Just watch though, I think she has been brought to heel but one never knows with spirit like that. Encourage her to go out with Katie. Give her some money to spend, take it from my drawer, but she does not ride alone!' he said grimly, then frowned suddenly lost in his own thoughts.

William watched with concern. 'What is it now?'

Richard ignored him for a few more moments. 'Do you know, I have the oddest feeling about this girl. I don't know why, but I think she knows something we don't know!'

William was alarmed. 'What makes you think that?'

Richard shook his head. 'I can't tell you,' he replied simply. 'It's my instinct, a gut feeling that tells me. There is something just a little more to Anne Howard than we think. She is deep, very, very deep indeed. She is the type who keeps secrets well, and my animal instinct warns me she has a secret from both of us but what it can possibly be I haven't the foggiest idea.'

William did not like this at all. 'Make her

talk?' he asked.

Richard bit his lip and shook his head. 'That would not be easy. I would have to shoot the mare, I guess, and I don't want to do that at all. No! She must just be watched very carefully—unless I'm getting like a timid old maid, and seeing ghosts under the bed!' he joked feebly.

William threw him a queer look. When Richard gave voice to a sentiment it made the older man pause with worry but he kept this to himself.

'I expect that is it!' he agreed a little too affably. 'You'll be throwing a fit of the vapours next!' he quipped with a smooth lie. The master came first, come what may. William knew if he had to choose he would not hesitate to kill the girl to save Richard Mason's life.

NINE

It was a superb night, warm, almost balmy and overhead. The sky was cloudless. The moon's brilliance was escorted by a multitude of stars, which winked down at Anne. They stilled some of the pain in her heart. She gazed upward with awe, wondering how many stars there were and how long they had been there.

She knew she was only putting off the evil moment of thought. She had decisions to make because today had been one of the worst in her life. She had run the whole gamut of human emotion, culminating in the stables' scene. Turning slowly, she sank in the big, leather chair and stared miserably at the opposite wall.

She realised she could not stay in this house now. Richard's behaviour, his iron stance, had shaken her foundations. It was true her disobedience had merited discipline, but the cruel, ruthless way he had been prepared to slaughter her mare was horrifically unbelievable.

How was it possible she had tasted true physical passion, yet half an hour later her feelings had changed to contempt, loathing and fear. She shook her head, confused, hurt and low.

This awful house with its multiple mysteries frightened her now. She let her thoughts drift back to the utter simplicity of country life even with its mundane boredom. Even the hardships and blows were better than this existence yet what, she asked herself, could she do? Where could she go?

She had tasted a little luxury and looked over at the robe in which hung gowns made to fit her with all the accessories any lady of the quality could want. She studied her soft hands, with their smooth skin; hands that were almost dainty, except for their large bone size. They were no longer a worker's hands, but appendages of idle luxury.

Her mind turned to Katie. She had been given a promise, which must be kept but what could two single females do to earn their living when they had no money? As far she was concerned, she was worse off than Katie. The maid looked her part, and would no doubt easily obtain a position elsewhere. Anne's only skills related to the countryside but what farmer would engage someone dressed in clothes of the quality with soft, delicate hands?

She still had the solitary gold coin given to her by old Lady Penford but that would take them nowhere. She could take her mare, which the two of them could ride double, to where? The future gaped with hostility, no matter how much she puzzled her brains, but staying in this house was just about out of the question. The sight of him would bring revulsion. The thought of his hand petting and touching her made her squirm. She had been stupidly blinded by a magnificent male body, bewitched by his caresses; and what if she were now pregnant? This was the second time this spectrum had loomed, and her shoulders sagged miserably. For the present she was trapped here, and she gritted her teeth. There had to be a way of escape, which meant she must bide her time and continue to think and think. Should she tell Katie? But she shook her head. Better by far to wait until something positive was on hand and in the interim she would continue here, but be very aloof and hostile to him.Thank God she had not told him about the eerie, left-handed swordsman. His likely reaction to this news and realisation of her eavesdropping made her blood curdle.

Katie had tapped on the door with a tray of food, but she had declined, knowing she must be alone with her thoughts. In the morning though, she would be expected to appear, and knew she must make the effort to act normally, no matter what it cost to her pride and dignity.

Her sleep that night was fitful. She heard sounds from the yard below, and, later, the clatter of hooves. She guessed it was that awful man going out again. At least she could always get her own back by informing the authorities he was a highwayman. It was with this pleasurable thought that she finally fell asleep. The idea she could exact revenge bolstered her bruised ego. Richard Mason was going to pay dearly, but she must be careful and wait. She must be clever.

She dressed immediately upon awakening and, with set face and pounding heart, walked down to the dining room. Jenny sent Katie in with her food and it was as if nothing had happened. No comment was made and Jenny did not even pass with a grin. Anne crinkled her forehead and considered.

It was true, everyone would know the master had been in a rage, but what had taken place in her room and the stables must be unknown to anyone else. Relief at this lifted her spirits a little. She managed a faint grin when Katie came in to collect the used dishes before she went to sort out her mistress's wardrobe.

Katie was relieved and knew Jenny was as well. They had both heard the thundering row from upstairs, but had exercised great tact and discretion. Lately, Jenny had not been quite so much an ogre. It was as if she had accepted Katie's new duties, or as if she had something more important on her mind.

'Hello ma'am!' Katy said brightly and handed her a pouch purse. 'William asked me to give you this from the master. It's money!'

With great suspicion, Anne peeped inside and gasped with shock. There must be at least twenty gold coins. Suddenly the future seemed a little more promising, but what was his game now? She struggled to remain straight-faced.

'Why didn't the master give them himself?'

Katie shrugged. 'He has gone away again and asked William to pass them over for you to go and buy yourself something, if you liked.'

Anne nearly snorted aloud. Conscience money, she told herself. There was enough here for her and Katie to leave without immediate worries. It still left the problem of exactly where to go, and she had enough wisdom to realise she must not act impetuously. Two lives depended upon her decision this time. She must think about it, make a very detailed plan, which incorporated her mare. He would be bound to come after her because she knew too much about his activities. She was too dangerous to be allowed to roam loose. She must seek distance and obscurity.

Anne lifted her head, aware of Katie's enquiring eyes on her. 'Katie,' she started carefully, 'I'm not going to spend this now. Do you remember what I promised?'

Katie held her breath, clasped her hands before her and nodded with excitement.

'Some time in the near future, I am going away, and you are coming with me, but it *must* be kept a secret. No one at all must know. If you tell anyone or even give a hint I would not be able to take you despite my promise!' she said evenly.

Katie's eyes opened wide with distress. The very idea of being left behind appalled her. Mistress Anne had given her life new meaning and she realised what Anne's statement meant.

'You mean I have to choose between you and the master?' she asked slowly.

Anne nodded, and waited, holding her breath. If Katie chose her master it would demonstrate where her loyalty lay, and she would feel free to talk to him about *that* night. She held her breath and waited with sharp worry.

'I pick you, ma'am!' she replied without

hesitation, and looked deep into Anne's eyes with sincerity and trust.

Anne let out her breath with relief, pulled the purse strings tight again, and handed it over. 'Here, Katie!' she said firmly. 'You take this and hide it somewhere very safe but where you can reach it a hurry. This money gives us our freedom for a new way of life. Do you understand?'

Katie took the purse and slipped it down the front of her bodice where it nestled comfortably between her small breasts. She nodded with eyes sparkling. Her trust complete.

'You must get a bag for our belongings and hide that as well. And after this morning we won't talk about this again for security.'

Katie nodded with complete understanding. 'Are we going for a walk? Good. I'll get us ready!'

Anne knew this was the best thing. Get out of this house for the time being, even if it meant walking in London's streets, which no longer appealed to her.

'And from now on, when we are alone together, I insist on you calling me Anne as if we were sisters. Agreed?'

Katie dimpled with pleasure. It was against her ingrained instinct, because, despite what she had just been told, familiarity would be untoward. On the other hand, her whole being cried out for closeness, a wanting to love and be loved. It was true Dan was showing an interest in her and she liked the quiet, stable man, but a female friend—her heart swelled.

'If you think that would be all right?' she asked hesitantly.

'I certainly do!' Anne grinned engagingly. Quite suddenly, the miserable morning was turning out much brighter than she had dared to imagine. Yesterday was not forgotten. It never would be but today held the promise of a future. 'That's settled then! Come on!'

'Right, Anne!'

They hastily left the house, both wearing their thinnest gowns, because already it was warm. It had not rained properly since she arrived, and the streets were thick with dust, constantly stirred up by passing horses. As they strolled Anne decided now was a good time to open the conversation in a specific direction.

'Who is Mr Wild, do you know?' she asked very casually.

Katie's face went sober, and she thought a bit before replying. 'I know him by sight very well, many people do and they talk about him. Some say he's a very bad man, and runs a horrible gang of thieves, but other people say he helps to control the crime.' She paused, wrinkling her forehead. 'If that is true, he can't be all that bad, can he?' she asked ingenuously.

'One would not think so,' Anne replied.

Neither of the girls was aware that a sullen

Joe followed discreetly at their rear. Never again would a female fool him. William had put the fear of God into him only yesterday.

'When Mistress Anne goes out, you'll follow and stick like a leech!' William had growled. 'You just lose her again and I promise, before I sack you without a reference, you will lose most of the skin on your back. Is that clear, boy?'

'Yes!' Joe had said between clenched teeth. Now he followed carefully, not allowing himself to be distracted by anything. He resented what had happened, and itched to get his own back, but knew he was powerless against his betters. Only gradually did it dawn upon him that by doing this he was away from William's erratic temper, leaving Dan working on his own. When this sank in, his mood lightened but, even then, he did not allow himself to relax his concentration. He knew William would do exactly as he had promised. Flay him alive with his large whip.

The girls halted at a street corner with their backs against a window displaying materials and Anne looked around, pondering deeply. She decided she did not now like London at all. It was simply too big, too noisy, too busy and too smelly for her taste. The sheen of novelty had eroded, and she could not help but make comparisons to country life. All these people walked and rode like automatons, going here and there, aimlessly, noisily, in a kind of ordered confusion. How naive she had been when she first arrived, and this had all excited her. Most of the men in carriages were fops, useless, powdered creatures, dainty and more effeminate than ladies. Her nostrils crinkled with distaste. Yes, she told herself, the sooner a situation arose, which gave the opportunity to leave the capital in safety she would not be sorry. She had tasted city life and found it badly wanting.

Her roving eye noted a carriage halt and a gentleman alight. His age was difficult to guess but his manner and distinguished bearing proclaimed him to be someone of substance and consequence. He wore a very fine blue coat edged with frothy, white lace. He carried a silver staff, a token of some important authority, and as he walked he inclined his head courteously to people. He acknowledged their presence and Anne found herself inclining her head in return. She noted Katie gave a polite bob, then shook her head ruefully. It was as if something baffled her.

'What is it, Katie?' Anne asked curiously.

'I don't understand it at all!' Katie replied with feeling in her voice. 'He looks so nice and is always so terribly polite to everyone!'

Anne turned to study the retreating back. 'Who is he?'

Katie stared. 'Of course! You've never met him before, but he's the person you asked about. Mr Jonathan Wild.'

Anne's eyes opened wide with astonishment. 'Him?' She gasped. Her mind reeled with incredulity, and she stared rather rudely. Surely, Katie was wrong? Her doubt showed in her expression.

'It is him,' Katy confirmed quietly. 'He is always like that in public. He never fails to nod to a female, whether she be of the quality or a servant like me,' she explained.

'Well I never!' was all Anne could manage. She was quietly thunderstruck. After what Richard had told her she had expected some vicious ogre. The man even had a kind face. He beamed at people benignly. When she thought of the left-handed swordsman there was no comparison. Jonathan Wild appeared to be a sweetie. Had Richard made a fool of her again? Yet, what profit was there in that? The puzzle gnawed at her, then suddenly, she understood in a flash of insight, nodding sagely to herself. Richard Mason was a ruthless highwayman, yet in London he appeared as a polished gentleman, touring the coffee houses. Who would ever suspect him? What better disguise for Mr Wild than to parade the capital's streets as a kindly soul, who nodded his head to ladies and maidens! In a way the two men were similar. Both were ruthlessly clever, masters of disguise, superb actors fooling the people at large. Her mind whirled with confused agitation. A short while ago she would have trusted her own judgment about anything but now, older and wiser from bitter experience, she realised she would never take anything again at face value.

Katie waited patiently for her wonderful new friend to rejoin her mentally. She was getting used to the moments when Anne became abstracted and removed from her. It never entered her head to probe or question, because she was far too happy just being with her adopted sister. She simply reached out and touched Anne's arm.

'I am wool gathering!' Anne said hastily; thank God for quiet companionship and sincere trust without questions.

For the rest of their walk, Katie noted that Anne asked no questions, and neither did she look around with interest. She understood that whatever it was that bothered her friend would be something she would learn in time. With that she was perfectly content. They strolled back to the house, Anne still quiet, immersed in whatever was on her mind and, as soon as they entered through the back door, Jenny met them.

'The master is back!' she announced importantly, before bustling into the kitchen from which came a variety of interesting smells.

Anne's heart sank and her lips tightened. 'I'm going to my room,' she said to Katie. 'I'll eat there if you can bring me a tray?'

Katie nodded. 'You are not riding today?'

Anne paused, debating. Not with him back. 'I think I'll check up on Night first though,' she said thoughtfully. Something prickled at the nape of her neck. She eyed the stable block and walked purposefully over. There did not appear to be anyone around, though she heard steps in the loft overhead. She walked down the passageway, and stilled abruptly as a chill went down her spine. Night was not there. She gasped and turned at the identical moment that Richard Mason appeared from a side room with William.

'Where's my mare?' Anne cried hotly.

Then two men exchanged an uneasy glance before Richard faced her, and Anne felt terrible fright.

'What have you done with her?' she shouted, almost hysterically.

From her eye's corner she noticed a brown horse standing with lowered head, very near the point of exhaustion. The saddle and bridle were on the floor nearby, ready to be taken for cleaning, and her eyes narrowed. The horse, a good one, had been ridden long and very hard. Sweat had cascaded down its body, leaving white streaks now drying slowly. The saddle girth was coated with a similar foam, as was the curb bit.

William picked up a nearby bucket, which steamed and walked past her to put it in the horse's manger. Anne's nostrils twitched with interest as she smelled linseed. She frowned

172

again. Horses were rarely given hot mashes at this time of the year, unless they had been under great strain. Her eyes dropped to the hooves. She knew this animal had recently been shod with new shoes yet here it stood with the toes worn thin.

She whipped around and stared hotly at Richard. 'What is going on here, and where is my mare?'

'Your mare is safe and well,' he replied quickly, a shade too fast he realised afterwards. William studiously ignored both of them. The horse had started to eat the hot mash and William was brushing away the sweat marks.

Anne bit her lip, consumed with worry, not trusting him at all. She glanced at his brown breeches, boots and coat. Casual colours, which would blend in anywhere except in a city. Her eyes travelled to his boots, and she was sure she could see dried sand under the instep. She swiftly tried to work out where the nearest seashore was but her geography was sketchy, especially regarding something she had never viewed.

He broke her silence. 'I would like to talk to you,' he said quietly.

Anne was inclined to ignore him, except that the mare's absence worried her desperately. A tremor played around her lips from agitation so slowly he took one of her hands and pulled her outside to the yard. They were alone now and could not be overheard.

'Look, I'm sorry you had a shock discovering your mare had gone. I intended to tell you, but you beat me to it. She is safe and well, that I promise!' he told her.

Anne lapsed into silence. She did not trust him one inch, feeling nothing but contempt for him, while she quaked inwardly. Why should her mare vanish? What was his dubious game now? She refused to look at him, and stared at the roof of the house with an indifference she did not feel. Did he dare to think she was going to fall all over him in a friendly way? His insolence was just about superb, but she would not co-operate.

He sensed her revulsion and understood. He realised why she kept her mouth shut and admired her self control. Other females would, by now, have been in a screaming fit of hysterics. This controlled aloofness aroused his genuine admiration. At the same time, he applauded, because it spoke well for his careful plan even if William did still disapprove.

Richard Mason took a deep breath. It was up to him to break this impasse. 'I am a bit tied up with business at the moment,' he started very carefully. Each word selected with precision. 'I also have some business elsewhere, and William has volunteered to do this for me. It means going away in the country and staying overnight at an inn. I wondered whether you would like to go for a change of scenery. It will mean a coach ride, but William will make all the arrangements. You know, I consider him completely trustworthy. As to your mare, I have borrowed her for a few days, because I might have need of a fast animal, and you said she was this. Not a hair on her will be harmed. That I vow!' and the tone of his voice held total sincerity. 'Please, just trust me for this once?'

Anne remained silent, suspicious of him, but examining every word he had uttered. For some reason, she knew she believed his trust concerning her mare, although she was deeply puzzled by this peculiar situation. She and William had reached a truce but a doubt arose as to whether he would really welcome her as a travelling companion.

He carried on hastily, disconcerted by her silence. 'I thought it would make a nice outing for you?'

Anne turned to face him. Her expression was implacable with hostility and her eyes narrowed thoughtfully. Suspicion bounced from her in a wave tangible enough to be felt by him.

'Katie?'

'Your maid will have to stay here. You can travel alone as William's niece. Then when you return, you can tell Katie all about the trip. Perhaps another time I can arrange an outing for you two girls only,' he told her blandly. She

175

simply *must* believe him. This climax had arrived just a little sooner than he had anticipated. Indeed, it was only by the grace of good fortune he had heard. Thank God there had always been enough money to pay his informers generously.

Anne had a shrewd idea he was lying in his teeth but for what reason she could not imagine. This man made no move without reason, and she was perfectly sure William did not wish any female's company on this business errand, let alone her. She studied him carefully. Was his face just a little too bland?

Richard read her with his uncanny knack. Of course she disbelieved him. If she had thought otherwise, he knew he would have been disappointed with her acuity but, on the other hand, he simply had to convince her. She hated him, there was no doubt about that, which was quite understandable. She was too controlled to fly at him. Any attack from her would be subtle. He allowed a slow smile to cross his face, without any idea how it changed him into that handsome Adonis.

'Anne!' he said gently. When circumstances warranted, he was capable of turning on a considerable natural charm. 'I do mean what I say. It is up to you, of course. If you would rather not have a trip on a coach, that's quite all right by me!' he lied with practised smoothness.

A coach, Anne thought. She had never been

in one, and her curiosity showed. Since coming to London she had seen them numerous times and watched fascinated, almost mesmerised— a huge vehicle pulled by four fine horses bred for strength and stamina as opposed to speed. On the front raised seat would be the coachman handling the four sets of ribbons, as she knew these reins were called. These were men of fame and skill, and they were looked up to like gods. Beside the coachman sat the guard with his blunderbuss. Inside the coach were the expensive fare passengers, surely people of the quality. If poorer people wished to travel, they had to huddle on the top exposed to all the elements, jumbled together with the baggage. There had to be something romantic about a coach. Her blood stirred with excitement; it would be a wonderful experience. There might never be a second opportunity in her life, because once she and Katie left here they would not have the money for expensive coach trips.

'All right!' she said a little ungraciously. Something still bothered her, yet he had given her the chance to refuse, and she eyed him again very carefully. Perhaps he did not have an ulterior motive. The journey might be genuine; it was a possibility, and obviously William must have agreed to her company. The day brightened a little more, as she considered swiftly all the angles but, try at she might, for the life of her she could find nothing sinister in his offer and no duplicity.

'I'll go,' she added a little more brightly.

He struggled to keep cool; relieved, glad, and scared all at once, but all he did was throw her a light smile.

'There is one condition though!' she said with very quiet firmness.

He stiffened uneasily. 'Which is?'

'My mare Night is to be here upon my return!' she bargained coolly.

'I promise you she shall indeed be here!'

'Then where is she now?' Anne shot back at him quickly.

He was nearly taken unawares. 'I can't say,' he replied simply holding his breath. 'She is well and that is the truth!'

Then why take her, Anne fumed to herself? She would not lower herself to argue with him, because, strangely, she really believed him this time. Night's disappearance was simply another of the oddities connected with his household and her resolve hardened a little more. The sooner she could shake the dust of this place from her and Katie's feet, the better.

'When?' she wanted to know adroitly, switching the subject. He might think her weak and too easily compliant if she kept on about her mare—even though her heart shrieked to know what was going on.

'The day after tomorrow!' he replied, and his features relaxed as a load shifted from his mind. He had known a refusal would have left him without a remedy, because he could not force an unwilling female to board a coach. 'Thank you, Anne. I will tell William. I think you will find he will be pleased to have your company!' he told her, meaning some of it.

Anne doubted this deep down, and slowly strolled back into the house and up to her room. She had deep thinking to do, because her instinct told her the whole thing was an absolute sham. But why? What possible reason could he have to invite her for a coach ride? It was crazy! What if she going mad? Had this house affected her wits and addled them?

Katie was thrilled for her, so Anne allowed her free rein to pick clothing, pack a small overnight bag and dress her hair on the morning in question. She studied the finished result carefully.

'Oh!' she murmured. 'You do look nice!' Katie complimented.

Katie had chosen a light-grey gown with dainty shoes to match. Anne's natural health and vitality, plus genuine rising excitement at the thought of the trip, had whipped her cheeks to a delicate pink. Her eyes sparkled and her neatly dressed hair finished a polished turnout. She studied herself in the glass. Where was the Anne of Yate? Who was this lady of the quality? It was madness, because she was still the same person inside. Take away these fine clothes, put her in an old gown and smock, dirty her hands and once again she would be a cowgirl.

'I wish you were coming with me, Katie,' she sighed. 'That doesn't matter. Just as long as you come back!' Anne sobered. 'I'll come back for you!'

'Do you know where exactly you are going?'

Anne gave a little shrug. 'I think we are going to travel east, but whether it is right to the coast I do not know.'

'I heard you are going by carriage to the coaching station,' Katie confided. 'I think Dan is driving you!'

They both heard heavy steps go along the passage and downstairs. They looked at each other. That would be William waiting tactfully below. Katie handed Anne a small overnight bag. Katie watched her leave the room, beaming with pride for her friend's adventure.

William waited near the bottom of the stairs. He never felt comfortable in town clothes, much preferring the free and easy garments of the stables. His mind was uneasy. Something heavy rested on his shoulders, which bothered him, so much so that, after considerable thought, he had deemed it prudent to take every precaution. He hoped to God the action would be unnecessary, but if not . . . he gave a little shrug to his shoulders.

He looked up, saw Anne Howard, and his eyes opened wide with amazement. My God! She was quite stunning! What a transformation good clothes and a superb hair arrangement could make. Who would have thought, only a short while ago, she had been ready to run him through with a pitchfork. This young lady, descending the stairs, would not disgrace a ballroom.

Anne was equally astounded as she halted and looked up at William. This well groomed man in such smart clothes could not possibly be the irascible bear from the stables? Not this scrubbed, closely shaved, highly polished gentleman with a refined air, who equalled any man of the quality. His boots had a dazzling sheen from polish. His shirt was beautifully white with elegant lace ruffles at the cuffs and neck. His hair was neatly slicked back, and from him came the entrancing odour of herbs.

'William!' was all Anne could manage at this incredible transformation.

He took her hand and surveyed her from top to toe, and then gazed into her eyes. 'You are a very lovely young lady, and don't let anyone tell you otherwise, at any time!' he complimented and meant every word.

Anne blushed, unexpectedly touched, taken aback at his sincerity. She took his proffered arm.

'Our carriage awaits us!' William explained.

'The master?' Anne wanted to know.

William gave a little shrug. 'Away on business again. You know what he's like by now!' He grinned engagingly.

Anne became aware of Jenny watching, an

expression of approval on her face. Anne grinned back, her heart lightening as she walked outside on William's arm, enjoying his solid masculinity.

William chuckled. 'If I were twenty years younger I think I would come a-wooing you!'

Anne knew she blushed and saw the twinkle in his eyes. William teasing? The world would stop next! The sun shone and her day stretched invitingly with excitement as he helped her into the carriage.

'Off you go, Dan!' William ordered. 'It's not all that far to the coaching station,' William explained, as she looked at the streets from a different angle.

At the coaching station, Anne's first impression was of violent, confused activity with horses everywhere. They were mostly of brown and bay colours and a standard make and shape. Tall, powerful animals with strong hocks and thick shoulders for pulling. Each horse was highly groomed and very corn fit. They danced from their stalls, flinging out kicks, sensing they would soon be working hard.They were backed into the coaches and shafts, with many assistants, and Anne saw the confusion was organised. Each man or boy had a set task, and did this without orders.

There were three coaches waiting with people standing to one side. One coach was ready, and the people climbed in, with only the luggage on the roof. The door was shut firmly, the coachman and guard climbed up, and the boys holding the horses' heads tensed, watching the coachman intently.

The horses ducked their heads, anxious to be off, and fidgeted impatiently.The coachman picked up his long, thin horn, blared his warning and nodded at the boys who jumped back skilfully. The four horses leaned against their collars to take the weight and the coach rumbled slowly into motion.

'Ours is over there!' William pointed.

Anne followed his gaze and turned to watch another coach leave. Three people climbed on the top to ride with the luggage. Then her attention reverted to their coach. The horses had been backed into the shafts, and men busily fastened the traces and chains. William took her arm and led her forward, ducking his head respectfully to another male traveller.

'My niece, sir,' she heard William explain. 'We are travelling for a short overnight stay. It is her first coach ride, and I think she is excited. Whether she will be after a few miles remains to be seen!'

The only other passenger, slightly taller than William, was leaner and lighter in build. He seemed to be roughly William's age and gave a rueful nod of agreement at William's words. Anne gave him a swift glance, noting smart clothes, just a little old-fashioned in their cut. She felt an insane desire to laugh. Fancy a cowgirl riding a coach.

'I think we will be travelling very light,' the other man said to William. 'This run has never been at all popular, especially at this time of the year.'

'Just as well,' William agreed. 'Coaches can be uncomfortable at the best of times, let alone when filled with six people.'

'I concur with you, sir. I think we should board. No poor people are obviously going on the roof—the lady . . . ?'

'Anne!'William said, drawing her attention from the activity, which held her fascinated. He prepared to help her inside as their travelling companion stood back for her, nodded, and very politely made a leg. Anne dimpled a pretty smile, inclined her head with equal courtesy, and somehow managed to stifle the giggle which arose again. It was suddenly important not to let William down.

They all settled inside, William and Anne together, their companion facing them in a corner seat. The door was shut, the horn blared imperiously as Anne's eyes sparkled with vivacity. Slowly, their coach moved forward, the iron-rimmed wheels grinding on the cobbles with a harsh clatter. She peered from her window seat, determined not to miss a thing.

The watching crowd parted hastily as the horn blared its strident warning, then they were out and moving at a steady trot. Anne was surprised how soon they had left the familiar built-up area, and she gazed about her, then gave a gasp as the coach's wheels hit a rough patch of road.

William threw her an encouraging grin. 'Coach riding can demand great fortitude!'

Their companion nodded a little dourly. 'A long ride can be a trial!'

Anne turned her attention to him. She noted his voice and speech with polished vowels but what was unusual? It was as if English was not his natural tongue or was it just that he came from another different part of the country? She wondered who he was, where he was going and for what purpose? What fun it was to travel and meet strangers.

The horses moved at a snappy trot. There were still a few buildings around, and the coachman kept sounding his warning horn but, as habitation was left behind, he ceased.

'Where do we change horses, do you know, sir?' the stranger enquired.

William turned and entered into a light, social conversation with him, while Anne's gaze reverted back to the window. They passed some cottages, with stretches of grassland in between, and now the coach's speed increased as the horses began to canter. The vehicle lurched and bounced on uneven portions of the road and Anne was forced to grasp the side strap to keep erect.

Then they were in the true country, and her eyes feasted on familiarity. This was her type of land; not the dirt, hustle and bustle of London. Here there would be peace broken only by the birds' dawn chorus or the lowing of the cattle. She was able to breathe in country smells again, soft and gentle, and, as she now understood, much loved by her. Somehow she and Katie must escape to rural tranquillity, come what may. No more cities or towns ever again.

The road was particularly rough now, and at their speed it was impossible to sit comfortably without bracing the body.

'I have heard news that a spring has been invented which will make coach travelling so much better,' William commented after two wheels hit a very bad dip and the coach swayed alarmingly before righting itself.

'It can't be too soon for me!' their companion replied with a grunt as they lurched a second time. 'Though when the coach masters will have all these fitted to their vehicles is another matter. I think it is the war that has slowed commercial modernisation down.'

'I agree with you, sir!' William told him. 'But surely the war will soon have to end?'

Their companion nodded. 'Wars bleed any country dry,' he agreed. 'I have heard that a grandson of Louis will be accepted as Philip V of Spain and that France and Spain will not unite against England!'

William snorted. 'All France has wanted

from the start is to rule the whole of the continent.'

'Is ambition bad though?' the other wanted to know.

William scowled at that. 'It *is* when Englishmen bleed and die. Look how our trade has suffered. It has stagnated because of the war!'

Anne switched her attention back to the scenery, disinterested in such a tedious, political discussion. From the window, she studied the countryside. She examined the height and depth of the grass, which was being grown for hay. The sun was delightfully warm, without being too hot, and it beamed down on the greenery. She spotted small patches of growing corn, which glowed a different shade of green to that of the grass. There were small herds of wandering cattle, and here and there, lone, solitary tracks weaved about. To one side was the sward of some wood and she felt a crazy wave of genuine homesickness, which was ridiculous.

The coach ride was dreadfully uncomfortable. Anne knew she had never been so jolted in all her life and she marvelled at the endurance of people who regularly travelled in this manner. Then their pace started to slacken. The hard bouncing eased and thankfully she sank back in her seat, wondering what was going to happen next.

The horses were back down to a slow trot,

then they dropped to a walk as they entered the yard of a large inn that appeared to stand in solitary isolation. Boys ran forward as Anne craned her neck. A new team of four fresh horses was already waiting, wearing their harnesses as the blown animals were swiftly unhitched and led away covered with sweat The new team was backed up with men working at top speed.

'They pride themselves on a fast change here. They are after the record!' the thin man commented.

'You travel this way often?' William asked casually.

'Now and again. It's never full. I don't quite know how they make a profit on this run.'

'Losses here will be covered by profits elsewhere perhaps?' William commented.

The fresh team were in position, the horn sounded and made Anne jump as the coach lumbered forward once more. William sat back in his seat and resettled Anne's little case which had jolted forward.

'That was The Bell!' William told her. 'A very good inn.'

Anne lurched as the coach wheels hit another abominable rut and swayed erratically again. All three of the travellers grabbed their support straps. The other man's small brown valise slipped to the floor and William leaned forward courteously to pick it up but its owner was quicker.

Anne had no idea how far they had travelled nor even where they were. She had to concentrate to try and find comfort, which was just about impossible. The coach's jolts were cruelly hard as the horses slowed again, and their sways were a little less frequent.

Once more, the scenery had altered, because the road now ran through a shallow valley, which was flanked on both sides by thick trees. The horses were now forced to walk as the coach wheels made hard work on ground still soft from damp and years of leaf mould.

Anne knew she was thoroughly disillusioned with coaches as a mode of travel. She had never imagined they could be quite so uncomfortable. A ridden horse was far superior, and she vowed never again to set foot in a coach.

Although the slower pace meant a little less jolting, she felt battered and bruised from their earlier speed. She turned to William to ask him a question and puckered her forehead. He had gone rigid, and the fingers of his left-hand beat a slow tattoo on the seat. The thin man also appeared ill at ease.

Anne turned back to the window, slightly amused. Surely a few trees, and the valley's more gloomy atmosphere was not quite so depressing? Then abruptly, the coach halted with a slithering jerk. There was an enormous bang, which shocked her, and everything

189

happened at once.

William leapt to his feet and flung his body before her, blocking her view.

'Highwayman!' he bellowed.

'The blunderbuss has been fired!' the thin man cried and struggled to stand, almost trembling with agitation.

The coach was canted to the left, leaning quite heavily, and Anne slid against the side.

'My niece!' William shouting with agitation, turning to the other man. 'Help me to protect her!'

Anne sat bemused, mouth agape, completely bewildered. From one eye corner, she could just see a horse and rider. The man was dressed all in black, with his face hidden by a mask. His horse stood quietly, while the robber held a pistol in each hand, with the reins tucked under his kneecaps.

Anne realised the guard had discharged his blunderbuss prematurely and was now unarmed. Her heart started to pound with fear, as William swung around, lurched against her, seemed to lose his balance completely, and cannoned into the other passenger.

He had been trying to stand straight, holding his valise with one hand, and at the same time pull something from his coat pocket. The highwayman heeled his well-trained horse two steps nearer.

'Everybody out!' he roared.

Both the coachman and the guard complied

with indecent haste as William and the thin man struggled to sort themselves out in the leaning vehicle. Anne sat frozen, frightened out of her wits, not knowing what to do at all.

The highwayman bellowed at the coachman and the guard. She just managed to see him waggle one pistol menacingly.

'Turn!' he snarled 'Keep running, if you want to keep breathing!' he threatened savagely.

The two men did not hesitate. They bolted in unison, and the tired horses stood quietly. Anne gazed with a hypnotised horror at the awesome highwayman. She had nothing of value. She flashed a look at William, who appeared to be engaged in some peculiar struggle with the thin man.

'Let me, sir!' William grunted, trying to take the other's valise. 'No! Don't touch it!'

'Then help me with my niece!' William cried. 'She is young and—!'

Anne was astonished. Although obviously they were in peril it struck her William was behaving in a panicky manner. She would never have thought this of him, then it hit her she was the cause. He was terrified for her safety.

'You people inside that coach—dismount!' the highwayman shouted at them.

There was no mistaking the ugly menace in his voice. William stilled and threw Anne a weird look, as his eyes flashed some kind of message. She gaped at him and struggled to understand. Then he paused a second to lean against her.

'Don't be afraid!' he hissed.

Anne blinked, broke her gaze from the two struggling men and shot a suspicious look at the highwayman.

'Get a move on in there or I'll send a ball in to hurry you up!'

'Quick, sir! Do as he says!' William cried urgently to the thin man.

'Damnation, no!' the strange man shot back, spittle flying from his lips with agitation. Then he moved with astonishing speed. He withdrew a very small pistol and raised it. Anne saw it was primed to discharge. She flashed a look at the highwayman and knew he was doomed at such close range. She flinched, ready for a second bang.

William let out one animal snarl of pure rage and flung himself forward. The pistol fired, making an incredible noise in their confined space and Anne jumped again. The highwayman spat out a foul oath and she caught her breath. Now she understood William's hissed message. Revelation was instant. Who would ever suspect a middle-aged man travelling with a young girl of being in cahoots with a highwayman. Richard and William had plotted this together, which meant this man had valuables in his valise. She had been the innocent disguise; used once more.

Her hurt, anger, and humiliation flared violently, and she turned to glower at William, then her heart missed two beats. William now leaned against the other man as their hands grappled but from William's front there showed a rapidly spreading red stain. As she gazed, William's movements slowed. Anne pulled herself up, trying to balance against the camber. She felt fear that something had gone badly wrong. She struggled with the door handle, and at last managed to swing it open with a thud.

'Richard!' she screamed in a panic. 'William has been shot!'

TEN

Richard Mason flinched, catching his breath with horror. How could disaster happen after so much careful, detailed planning? He gritted his teeth with anguish. The unexpected, the unforeseen, the one factor beyond calculation, because it was the quantitative unknown . . .

He aimed one pistol inside, and the thin man spun around, holding William's sagging body as a shield, while his eyes were ablaze with fury at the trap. Clever as he was, careful to calculate a move before he made it, he had been fooled by the girl's apparent naive innocence. His guard had been let down too soon and here was death. Worse, everything for which he and many others had planned and laboured now stood open to a disclosure with horrific consequences if the valise was opened.

'The valise!' William managed to grunt. 'Get it, Anne!'

'Don't you dare touch it!'

'Grab it, Anne!' Richard bawled at her.

For a second she froze at the variety of commands. William gave one gigantic heave, and hurled the thin man aside. He kicked the valise with accuracy, and it shot through the open door. The thin man went berserk. He ducked under William's hand and faced a terrified, bewildered Anne. Her eyes were wide open, flaring white as she took in the gaping hole in William's chest, through which blood now pumped very fast. William sagged back on the seat, a beseeching look thrown at Anne.

She snapped into action. As the thin man vainly tried to catch the valise before it hit the ground, she stuck out one foot. He lost his balance, tripped and fell headlong from the coach in a tangle of arms and long legs. Anne whipped around and leaned towards William, holding a strap to retain her balance.

'Oh William!' she groaned, horrified at the blood he was losing.

He looked up at her, a queer smile twisting his lips. 'That has sorted out Abbé Gaultier once and for all!' he grated with satisfaction, then coughed heavily and the blood flowed faster.

'William! William!'

His lips moved as he stared up into her distressed eyes and forced up some last dregs of strength.

'Anne! Listen to me!' he panted. 'I'm dying so I can only say this once. Pay attention!'

'Yes! Yes!' she gasped, and took one of his huge hands between hers as tears welled. This great bear of a man strained to suck air into tortured lungs.

'Richard might face another danger! There is also the letter!!'

'What letter?'

He managed a feeble nod, coughed and more blood spewed over her hands. 'Go to my room, get the letter, read it and tell him when you think fit!'

'Letter in your room?' Anne gabbled frantically, desperate, terrified as she saw life prepare to leave him.

'Hidden! Look! Use your common sense. I was wrong about you, girl! Look after Richard. Watch his back. Protect him because—!'

He heaved and another flow of pink, frothy lung blood poured from his mouth. 'Letter!' he managed his last word.

'Yes! Yes! Letter but where?'

Then he slumped and died. 'Richard!' Anne screamed frantically.

She saw he had dismounted, thrown the reins over one muddy coach wheel and clutched the valise in one hand. Of the thin man, there was no sign. He scrambled into the leaning coach and stood, slack jawed with disbelief. His shoulders heaved and tears appeared. Anne had never seen a man cry before and she felt as if she was intruding upon something terribly private. She bit her lip and averted her gaze tactfully.

Then he collected himself.'Where is that damned Frenchman?' he cried.

Gaultier had always known when discretion was better than valour, and his long legs had swiftly propelled him to the cover of the trees. Swearing foully, he bolted for his life and also to issue a general warning though it was highly unlikely this could be in time. Better to save his own skin to fight another day.

Richard helped Anne down from the coach, clutching the precious valise tightly. For a few seconds he clutched her in his arms, feeling her wild trembles.Thank God she was not the fainting, screaming hysterical kind, otherwise he would have been forced to leave her.

'Sshh! Sshh!' he crooned as tears cascaded down her cheeks. 'Try and control yourself!'

Slowly Anne obeyed and wiped her face with a bloody hand. She looked up at him, confused and going into shock. 'Come! We must get away from here quickly!'

Anne looked up at the coach. How was it

possible that in under one minute, a vital, powerful man could die? Dear irascible William. She threw him a silent question.

'We have to leave urgently,' he told her heavily. 'The two who ran will soon get their courage to come back. We must get as far away as possible!'

He opened the valise and peered inside. Anne did too, expecting valuable jewels but all she could see were papers of some kind. Richard pulled some out and rapidly scanned them, then grunted with satisfaction. He gave a nod.

'William has not died for nothing!' he growled.

Anne shook her head. 'I don't think I will ever understand anything again,' she said with considerable feeling. She looked at herself; she was smothered in William's blood.

'It's a very long story, and here is neither the time nor the place to tell it. We must get shelter for the night. It's macabre, but I had an ominous feeling something might just go wrong. I never expected—this!' and he nodded up at the leaning coach, which now held William's body. 'That is why I brought a second horse, the very best.Yours! She is tucked away in my hiding place.'

'Night!' Anne gasped.

'I picked her just because of what you said about her speed,' he explained grimly. 'We might end up needing that too!'

Anne shook her head helplessly. There were no words left, no questions, just a void of pain and shock. 'It seems wrong to ride away and leave William like that!' she protested.

Richard faced her and closed the valise. 'He would understand and approve!!' Then he passed the valise to her and scrambled back into the coach and went through William's pockets. He removed a few small articles, which he placed in a kerchief, knotted it, then slipped them into a pocket before dropping back down to her.

'We must hurry,' he told her simply but his words vibrated with barely restrained urgency. 'We cannot tarry here. I will mount you behind me for the time being! Now we must go! There is going to be an enormous hue and cry about this!'

He bent and studied the grass with the bent fronds, trampled stones and patches of clinging, muddy earth.

'See that rock over there!' he pointed. 'Get up on it and you'll find it easy to mount behind me. Then we will ride on all the hard stretches, because no one must guess my horse carries double. I know a stream where we can also ride to foil hounds.'

Anne gave him a wan look. She shivered badly now from shock, so he took her arm and helped her climb up, then returned for his horse. He tied the valise firmly to a D-ring on his saddle, then he took the time to reload his pistols and put them in their saddle holsters. He mounted, rode over to the rock, kicked one foot free from a stirrup so she could use it as a step. While she mounted and settled herself behind the saddle's cantle he waited grimly—fully alert, but with a very heavy heart. Never in a thousand nights had he envisaged William's death would be like this. Both of them had considered the possibility of some complication, which was why they had decided upon the black mare. Never before had the Abbé Gaultier been known to use a pistol, or even carry one. The fact he had today had shown the other side's general desperation. He licked his lips.There was always the chance that Gaultier had allies in this region who would rally to his call, then he and Anne would become the hunted. He threw a worried look at her over his shoulder. He also knew that when the opportunity arose she was going to throw a barrage of questions at him. She certainly had the right now.

Anne settled herself, as well as she could. and put her arms around his waist for balance. Her mind jangled with what she had witnessed and William's final words only added to the most horrible confusion. What letter? And where was it? Why had William managed to look so self-satisfied, even smug, when he was dying? Who exactly was this mysterious Gaultier? And why had William said she was to tell Richard when she thought fit? Tell him what and when?

Her head swam as questions hammered at her brain. She felt weak and helpless. She simply wanted to find a long, dark hole, crawl down it, curl up in a ball and let the world drift by to leave her in peace.

He was sensitive enough to realise she was near the end of her tether. 'Courage!' he murmured to her as he guided his horse skilfully on all the hard ground he could find before making it enter, then wade, up a stream. 'It will all look different in the morning, though you may not think so right now,' he encouraged.

Anne had no words nor the energy to think of any. She simply sat, acquiescent, swaying in time with him. After a short while, he moved into a slow canter, and they rocked together. This seemed to go on for hours and hours and, at one stage, she knew she had nodded off lightly. She awoke, when the horse came back to a walk to enter another stream, which was deeper.

She could feel the play of the muscles on his back and his masculine sweat. She was also conscious of his mental alertness; the feeling he was awake and ready for any danger assuaged her own utter incompetence.

Evening came, and still he rode along while she now dozed, resting on his back. Richard Mason rode with every nerve highly alert for action. He kept a careful watch on his horse's ears for a warning of another horse's presence. He could feel the girl slumped against him and guessed she was asleep, so he dare not trot.

The first star showed as he arrived. He stopped his horse and looked around warily, scenting the air like a hound. The ears of his horse flopped forward, all relaxed as he moved in his saddle.

'Wake up!' he whispered. 'We have arrived. Can you dismount without help?'

Anne, nodded, then realised he could not see this. Holding him for support, she slid her leg over the animal's quarters and landed on her toes, stumbling once. He sprang down after her, taking her arm anxiously.

'You are all in!' he said, and sighed. 'We both are but first things must come first. See! It's an isolated woodman's hut. I discovered it a long time ago, quite by chance. It is never used, I think it has been forgotten. Your mare and my best horse are hidden in their little dell nearby. This horse is, shall I say, borrowed!' he explained with a lift of his eyebrows. 'Once I've checked the other two are safe, I'll let him go. He will find his own way back home in time!'

'If he is not stolen again!' Anne managed to quip with an effort.

'Good girl!' he encouraged. 'The hut is good as a shelter. It's even quite dry. There is a cauldron in it, and a small spring on the left. Fill it so you can wash, then let me have your gown. I'll bury both of our sets of clothing. Thank God, I always come prepared for all eventualities,' he said, then halted. Well, not quite all, he added to himself grimly, but aware she watched him, he forced a lighter look on his face. 'I've spare clothes, which you could wear as well as a change for myself.'

'Where are they?' she wanted to know, as she fretted now to discard everything which had William's blood.

'Where our best saddles are. You get water, while I check my gear and our best horses. I shan't be long.'

Anne looked around. The trees were thick, the hiding place just about impossible to spot even with a steady stare. She quivered internally, yet her instinct told her she was safe.

She investigated the hut, which was as he described, while he took the horse in the opposite direction to that which they had ridden. He was back very shortly, and he took the cauldron from her, carrying it back inside, with one hand, while the other held a pair of saddlebags.

'Strip and wash, for both of us, then I'll hide these dreadful clothes,' he told her as he dived into one saddlebag, pulling out shirt, breeches, hose and a short dark brown coat. 'These should fit you!' he explained, while he stripped off his own black clothing.

Anne felt no embarrassment at stripping before him. After the day's experiences, she knew nothing much could ever trouble her again. She washed hastily, but thoroughly, shivering at the cold water, then backed out of the way for him. She dressed more slowly, finding the boy's clothes unusual but also comfortable. When he too had donned fresh clothes he picked up their soiled garments.

'There is bread and dried meat in the other saddlebag. I won't be long. I know an old badger's sett, where I can hide these and block it up with some rocks. No one will ever find anything!'

Again he was swift as she sat on a three-legged low stool, arms crossed over her breasts, her mind a blank. He was back in no time, took one look at her and recognised full-blown shock. With quick fingers, he found his emergency rations, divided them out, watched her chew slowly.

He then displayed two old cloaks and put them down. 'The floor is a bit uncomfortable. It is only earth, but it's dryish and better than being outdoors. Try to sleep. No talking tonight!' he advised, as he checked and loaded his pistols, bolted the rough-hewn door and placed his weapons alongside his cloak.

Anne was thankful to lie down as her legs had started a ridiculous trembling. She knew she could never sleep after such a day but as she lay her head down on an upturned saddle for a pillow, she went out as if pole-axed. Shock acted to slow her system for recovery.

She awoke with a violent start, her wits whirling as she gazed up at the roof and struggled to puzzle out where she was and why. Then memory returned with a violent rush, which made her gasp. She turned and saw him lying beside her, still asleep, although nerves twitched in his throat and neck. He had obviously been restless, because his shoulders were bare so, carefully, she pulled the cloak's edge over him.

She put her hands behind her head and started to think. What an awful day, yesterday had been. Was it really true that William was dead? Part of her mind had to grapple with facts, to understand. She saw him slumped against the coach seat, blood pumping from the ghastly chest wound as he fought to live a few more seconds to talk to her.

Once again, his words seared into her mind for all time, reverberated with as little sense as when he had gasped them out. What could he have meant when he said she was to tell the master only when she thought the time was right. What time? What could be hidden in a letter? Her spirits slumped. When she returned, this would mean going through William's room in absolute secrecy. She knew this would feel like a trespass but she had promised the dying man.

The London house! Yesterday changed everything! How could she think about her and Katie riding away to leave Richard alone now? It would be cruel in the extreme. She pictured him again, when tears had flowed down his face. What sorrow to make a man cry; what great love he must have had for William. This explained why William had so often issued the orders. They had been brothers as much as in the flesh.

Anne examined her own feelings. Her hatred and contempt for him had flown. Some plan had obviously gone hideously wrong, and though she had been a kind of bait, this no longer rankled. Her feelings for him, the arrogant, dominant way he had treated her were explained by the dangerous life he led. How petty her past feelings had been, she thought as she watched dawn slant pink fingers of light through the cracks in the hut's rough wooden planking. He was a criminal. If caught, he would be hanged.Yet yesterday had touched her heart. A man who grieved like that before a female could not be wholly bad. Perhaps this last robbery was to be his final one? She clutched at this fragile straw of hope but what would happen when they returned to his house? A hundred questions hammered at her now and she failed to find one logical answer.

His breathing changed and he awoke quickly. He lay quite still, but his honed senses were alert. He could feel her eyes upon him, but he lay still, listening, scenting, relying upon his instincts, which had saved him in the past.

As soon as he was sure they were safe, he relaxed on his back and put his own hands behind his head to gaze upwards.

He was gone! Dead! Finished! It was all over! He set his jaw, determined not to break down again. They had succeeded, but surely it would be acknowledged the price William had paid was too high? How could he ride back into that stable yard, and not be met by William's gruff, cheery voice? He knew now he had reached some awesome crossroads in his life.

The girl had been brilliant. He had thought her backbone was good, but had never imagined it was constructed from such fine steel. The way she had acted yesterday! He marvelled with wonder. No faints or screams. She had tried her best to help and tripped Gaultier. She had ridden away from William's body and spent the night here with him without question or fuss. He examined his feelings for her. A life with Anne by his side would be an incredible experience. He dared to wonder if she had forgiven him for his past harshness. Did she carry resentment in her makeup? He knew today he would have to find out.

'He taught me how to tickle trout!' he told her softly, turning. Anne rolled on her side and faced him. Pity welded in her heart at the bleak sadness on his face.

'He was always there. I cannot remember

my father. It was always William!'

'You loved him very much?' she said with gentle understanding.

He lifted a hand and held it out to her beseechingly. His heart strained and croaked as his eyes filled with misery. Damn! He had vowed not to show tears again, but the empathy in her eyes was too much for him.

Anne wriggled nearer, leaned over and placed his head on her breasts. 'Sshh!' she whispered, comforting him in the only way she knew how. 'Remember all the good memories. Think of the good times. William was a strong man. He would approve of a period of mourning, but would become impatient and scorn a long variety.'

He was awed at her sudden wisdom and looked at the warmth in her eyes, the tenderness of her mouth. Her breasts were soft and warm and parting the shirt's folds, he felt a nipple as his loins stirred. He paused to check her eyes, but they glowed warm and encouraging, her lips held an understanding smile. Like the great earth mother, she knew her body was the one priceless gift to offer at such a time.

She delicately wriggled out of her clothes as he slid from his breeches, then she was in his powerful arms. He stopped once again, to make quite sure he was welcome, and she lifted a hand to stroke the nape of his neck. She arched her body invitingly as he moved into her—slow, considerate and grateful. How could one so young show such superb wisdom? Their lovemaking was the soft, gentle kind in which each strove to please the other. They had all the time in the world and knew it. They climaxed on the same high wave and, when they were finished, he rolled on his side, still holding her and stroked her hair.

Finally, he turned away. 'This won't do!' he said slowly.

Anne felt replete and satisfied. 'I feel I could stay here forever!'

'I wish that life would let us. However, we will have today. One precious day alone!' he promised.

'And then?' she asked in a soft voice. 'We cannot hide forever!'

His mind slid into its usual intelligent, alertness. He was conscious of her eyes upon him, waiting patiently.

'No!' he agreed. 'Tomorrow we will go back and I will explain everything to you, but not today. I think I would like to spend some hours in the Dell with the horses. It's a soft gentle, kind place, hidden from eyes, probably unknown, because there are only animal tracks around. I would just like to sit and think back. I want to turn over memories. I want today to be my memorial for William,' he explained a little anxiously.

She understood and was relieved. A return to London, immediately after yesterday, would have been an unbearable strain. Tomorrow was another dawn. She looked at him inquiringly, as he stood and hastily dressed. He carefully checked his pistols and buckled on his sword and belt and hefted one pistol thoughtfully. She rose and copied him and waited for him to speak.

'Can you light a fire in that old hearth there? You will find kindling at the back of this hut and over there is a tinder and flint. Put the cauldron on to boil and stay hidden until I return,' he said, handing the pistol to her. 'I'm sure there's no one around, but it is wise to be prepared at all times. You fire this pistol by pressing here. Be careful, it's ready to use. If anyone should try to get in, while I am absent, fire at the belly, which has the greatest target. Do you think you could do this?'

Anne swallowed and took the weapon gingerly. It felt strange, heavy and lethal. She bit her bottom lip, but nodded.

'I'm going to check on the horses then I'll see if I can catch our dinner. I never travel without this!' he said triumphantly, producing his sling. 'With any luck, we will have a stew of coney for our supper tonight.'

He filled the cauldron for her, and once he had gone Anne carefully bolted the door and with the kindling he'd also brought in, she started a fire and sat on the ground, the pistol her hands. She hoped she would not have to use it, but she suspected she would not hesitate. Once she had the fire going, there was nothing else to do. The kindling and sticks were quite dry, so there was only the tiniest plume of smoke drifting up through the ceiling cracks.

Dear Richard! Then she stopped to examine herself. Only a few days ago, she had loathed him! She examined herself carefully. It struck her with a hammer blow that her softening for this man was but a prelude to her admission of love for him. Yesterday morning she had been a simple girl. Today, she felt like a bloodied warrior, and her expression became grim. There was no going back, but what did he feel for her, apart from desire for her body? They were poles apart socially, because Anne knew she could still be sensitive about her illegitimate status and menial upbringing. He was very well bred, very much of the quality, superior to her with education and social graces. It was true, given half a chance, she could catch up rapidly. Would he one day become bored with her? Would he despise her background? Then it occurred to her, he already knew it so why worry? She heard something outside and went stiff.

'It's me, Richard!' he said in a low tone.

With a sigh of relief, she scrambled up to let him in, glad to pass the pistol back. He beamed at her, one large coney in his hands. He had already skinned and gutted it and now he swiftly jointed the carcase and popped it into the cauldron with some herbs that he had gathered and wild onion tops. He swiftly sorted through some logs to place them in strategic positions.

'We'll be ready to eat that tonight. Until then we manage on dry rations. Come on, let's go to the horses!' he told her and took one of her hands in his. She trotted after him as he led the way down a tiny path flanked with tall, thin grasses under towering trees. She stepped into a tiny glade, where his best brown horse and her black mare grazed happily together, restrained by hobbles. The grass here was lushly rich, and on one side a tiny stream tinkled along, brisk and merry.

'The tack is behind that bush!' he pointed.

'What a lovely spot!' Anne whispered, quite entranced with its simple beauty and natural peace. She walked forward, bent and scooped a handful of water from the stream. It tasted cool and sweet. On one side, the trees nestled close together, and he led her to a slightly higher spot with a grassy bank. It made a perfect seat.

They sat together in silence, neither finding the need to talk. It was good summer's day, and the sun's rays were muted by the overhead leaves. The only sounds came from the birds, insects and munching horses. The air was sweet, like the water, and Anne felt a great peace envelop her troubled spirit.

Yesterday was blanked out. It had not gone

completely, but the events, worries and questions were shelved. Contentment flooded her, soft and balmy, soothing jangled nerves and when he put one arm around her shoulders, without speaking, she felt enormously comforted.

The two horses crunched amicably together, taking little steps, because of their hobbles.Their teeth made a soothing sound. Now and again they swished their tails together.

'It's fairy like!' she whispered.

Richard turned to her. He was deeply troubled, filled with barely controlled grief, still in a state of disbelieving shock. Only yesterday morning, at this time, William had been alive. How could a man's life alter in seconds? Then he berated himself. He should know. When a man lived with danger, life became a cherished commodity. As they sat, he had reviewed his past life, reassembling facts; with his vast experience he was able to work out what would happen next. Tomorrow he would tell her.

'You have not asked one question.Yet, you must be brimming with them!' he murmured to her, and gave her a squeeze.

Anne smiled at him, soft and gentle. 'That's true!' she agreed. 'But not today. Don't let's spoil this tranquillity,' and her voice tailed off. She had a suspicion that when he did talk there might be matters that would disturb her.

He nodded at the horses. 'There is no one

around. They are so relaxed!'

' The best sentinels we could have!'

So they sat throughout the day. He handed her the last of the dried meat, while the Dell's life accepted them because of their silence and stillness. The birds settled down. Some woodland butterflies appeared. A coney showed itself cautiously, studied them for a few seconds, then gave itself a quick toilet. A fox trotted into view, threw them a surprised look, halted with one paw uplifted before finally trotting brazenly before them intent upon his own business.

Gradually, the sun moved down to the West and the day creatures started to vanish. Early night moths fluttered among the trees as the birds' noises ceased. The horses stood with heads hanging low and relaxed, each resting a hind leg on a hoof tip, tails gently moving.

'It's been magic!' Anne told him in a low tone. Noise would be a blatant intrusion. 'I will never forget this place, or today!'

'Come!' he said, standing. They were both a little stiff. 'Our stew should be ready, and I'm hungry!'

Anne noted how he changed. Once more, he was alert, head tilted as he listened and studied their surroundings. He led the way slowly, padding silently back to the hut with her at the rear. His eyes were everywhere. He stood a few seconds before approaching the hut, allowing his senses full rein and relaxed a little. They were still alone and safe.

As they stepped into the hut, a delicious aroma wafted to them. The fire was nearly out but the cauldron's contents had been evaporated down to a thick mush of goodness. He quickly fed the fire while Anne hunted around and found two old flat dishes to serve as platters. They were not particularly clean, but they were both too hungry to be fastidious. They had no cutlery, so they used their fingers.

When their bellies were satisfied, he went for more water, and they settled down for the night together. They undressed and admired each other's bodies, and went to each other automatically. The moon gave a little glow through the cracks of the walls and the low fire added a tinge of colour as they made love again.

It was the birds' dawn chorus that awoke them simultaneously and they lay together each now thinking unhappily, of what was to come. He stroked her face, looked deep in her eyes and a half rose on one elbow.

'I have fallen in love with you,' he admitted. 'Will you marry me?'

Anne lay still, not expecting this so soon.

'Would that be wise?' she asked gently. 'You are better bred and educated than myself. I know who my father was but nothing about my mother.'

He gave a snort. 'I want to marry you. I don't give a damn about breeding. It proves nothing. In many ways I think we are two of a kind. I think we could be excellent partners for each other!'

'Your—work?' she asked nervously.

He had guessed this would come out.

'That was merely a cover which I will explain later. I am an espionage agent and that man in the coach is my opposite number. We have repeatedly tried to kill each other and failed!'

Anne could not have been more flabbergasted if he had said he was from the moon. 'But—?'

'Tell you all tomorrow so will you be my wife?'

She nodded, eyes as round as saucers. 'Of course I will! But not too many shocks please!'

ELVEN

She was delighted to be on her mare once more. While he mounted she studied the little hut with great affection. The spare saddle they had hidden, although they both knew it would deteriorate without attention.

He joined her and grinned engagingly. 'I only had one kiss this morning,' he complained.

She shook her head reprovingly. 'That's because today is for business. I have a

215

suspicion you have a lot to tell me?'

He nodded heavily. 'I will talk as we ride back towards London. I can start by saying, I am pretty certain the highwayman's days have ended, thank God. It served a useful purpose, which enabled me to move around everywhere. Indeed, if everything goes right, and I pray to God this will be so, I can leave London. We would not have to live in the capital if you fancied somewhere else.'

'I am very disillusioned with the city,' Anne admitted, 'and I would not fancy spending the rest of my life there. Oh! When I first came it was also strange and exciting, a pure novelty, but not any more. I realise now I am a true country girl, through and through. My idea of a home would be somewhere in the country, where there is green grass, sweet air, and animals around me. I like animals. They are so uncomplicated. They are relaxing.'

Richard took all this in and nodded to himself. 'That certainly suits me. I have never been a lover of London or any urban development. So that's it then. I'll find us a place in the country. I am quite well off moneywise and the present house was only leased. Incidentally, the money I have does not come from theft, so there would be nothing to trouble your conscience,' he grinned.

'What happened to us before?' she asked quietly. 'I thought I hated you at one stage,' she admitted heavily, 'after what you threatened to do to Night—' and her voice tailed off in confusion.

'Yes!' he replied with a great sigh. 'That was all unfortunate, but when I've told you my tale, I think you will agree. I simply could not have you jeopardising your own safety, because it would have rebounded on me and William. You will have guessed it was vital you travel with William as innocent cover. It fooled Gaultier all right. We have crossed each other a number of times in the past, and I never knew he carried a small pocket pistol,' and he shook his head unhappily.

Anne eyed him sternly. 'Would you have killed Night?' It was vital she knew.

He hesitated, then knew only the truth would do. A lie between them now would do irrevocable harm, because she would be sharp enough to see through it. He braced himself.

'Yes!' and awaited the storm.

Anne nodded to herself. 'That's what I thought,' she replied quietly. She had wondered if he would be honest, and knew that if he had lied her feelings for him would have been fatally doused with icy water. He had been brave and honest enough to be truthful, which laid a firm foundation for their dual emotions. Her heart glowed for him as he kept a steady look deep into her eyes as if trying to read her thoughts.

'And I will be your wife,' she paused. 'There might be pitfalls though,' she added with

217

shrewd wisdom. 'We both like our own way. If your family—!'

'That is something I cannot discuss at the moment,' he said, pulling a face. 'I have a reason for this. A terribly important one. Later on in the year I will be able to explain but for the time being you must accept me as I am. I can say both of my parents are dead, and as you know, William reared me, and at the end he held you in very high regard.'

'He did?' she exclaimed. This knowledge pleased but also saddened her.

'So, you will marry me towards the end of the year?'

Anne nodded. 'I will!' Perhaps her background truly was of no consequence to a man who must have killed. Richard sometimes appeared to be his own law, and certainly a life with him would not be dull. She had a pretty good idea too that he would not stray from the matrimonial bonds. In his makeup loyalty had been inbred. He would cleave to her, protect her, give her excellent children and make a first-class mate. Money was of no consequence to her at this stage. It was true, she was still a minor in law, but who cared about her to argue this point. She only had him—and Katie—and if his plan to leave London matured the future would be ideal.

'I have been a political espionage agent for a long time. I started as a member of the Duke of Marlborough's team working for England against France. William's killer, the Abbé Gaultier is certainly my opposite number. How we have not managed to kill each other before now is a mystery, because we have clashed often enough.'

Anne shook her head. 'I think you have started in the middle of a story. Can't you go back to the beginning?'

He nodded. 'I suppose it all starts with King James II, and his harsh policies against the Protestants. He foolishly allowed attacks to be made upon Anglican bishops so certain people invited his son-in-law to be king instead. He was William of Orange. King James II was forced to flee England, and live the rest of his live in exile. He did make one try to come back through Ireland when his revolt failed. All right so far?'

'Yes, I understand all that!'

'So, so we had King William on the throne with his wife Mary as his joint, equal ruler. Not as a consort.'

Anne interrupted. 'How was that possible?'

He picked his words, to enable her to understand. 'William was the nephew of King James II while Mary was his daughter. Both of them had a legitimate claim upon a throne so, as they were married, each became a ruler, which happened in 1689. Now in 1701 we had the Act of Settlement, which made it impossible for any Catholic to be a monarch again. This was because of the Catholic Queen we call Bloody Mary. This was fine, except for one snag. William and Mary did not manage to rear a living heir. So the crown went to our present Queen Anne, who is another daughter of the exiled James II. The problem now is that she has no living heir and is a pretty sick woman. She could die at any time. This has caused great worry, because where do we find an heir to the throne, who is not Catholic?'

Anne listened fascinated. 'So what is going to happen?'

'Trouble!' Richard replied grimly. 'You see, the exiled King James II happened to have a son and he has claimed the throne but he is a Catholic!'

'Oh!' Anne said significantly, as she began to understand the problem.

'He also happens to have a certain following in England!' he paused. 'All those parts which have a strong Jacobite following. These Jacobites are sworn followers of James II, and they are all Catholics, and usually Tories. They have made a lot of trouble and agitation in the past. This did die down for a bit when William and Mary were on the throne, but it has all started up again now that Queen Anne's poor health is common knowledge. The Jacobites are flexing their muscles to put their pretender—they call him James the Third—back on our throne and turn us into a Catholic country once more. This cannot be allowed because it would only lead to another civil war.

Look at the dreadful loss of men in the civil wars just over sixty years ago, when it was the royalists against Parliament. Father fought son; brother tried to kill brother. It was a dreadful time in our history and the country would be in turmoil again. We have many enemies, just waiting in the wings for the rich pickings of our trade to fall into their hands,'

'So what is going to happen?' she asked, deeply interested. She realised how totally ignorant she was of such matters. This was where her country living made a debit mark. People in London would have the credit of being constantly up-to-date.

His horse bounced and gave a little impatient buck so the black mare copied; both horses objected to this slow pace. They wanted to stretch their legs in a gallop.

'The important Act of Settlement said the next person to inherit the throne must be the issue of Sophia of Hanover, the Electress, because all of that line are dedicated Protestants.'

Anne was bewildered with this strange name. He saw her puzzled frown, and hastened to explain. 'King James the First, father of the exiled James the Second, had a granddaughter, who is Sophia, Electress of Hanover, by marriage, so here is a direct line to the throne.'

Anne mulled this over and worked it all out. How complex the whole matter was. 'So it boils down to the fact there are two claimants to the throne. One is Protestant through Sophia, while the other is Catholic through James the Second. Is that correct?'

'Spot on!' he grinned. She had a quick brain, and now her bright eyes were fixed upon him but she chewed her lip as something entered her head.

'Well it's obvious what should happen,' she said firmly. 'Just let them fight it out!' she stated with female practicality.

Richard chuckled at this. 'Impossible! Don't forget the Act of Parliament as well as the present war!'

Anne snorted at this. 'I never did understand what the war was all about in the first place. What do country people like me know about what happens at court in London?'

Richard shook his head quickly. 'No, Anne! Not the court!' he rebuked gently. 'Parliament! It is Parliament who rules, the monarchs merely reign, and there is a vast difference, thank God! Although you think Parliament is disinterested in your little village, you are very wrong. She is concerned, most desperately, because of trade. Commerce affects everyone!'

Anne shook her head and rolled her eyes. She knew she was out of her depth, and he could see this and hastened to explaining greater detail.

'The war itself is about succession to the

throne. It began because King Louis the Fourteenth of France wanted to put *his* man on the throne of Spain when *their* king died without issue. If we had allowed this to happen, France would have ended up with most of the continent. England would have been placed in a highly dangerous situation and other countries the same.'

'Which other countries?' Anne shot at him, frowning again.

' Prussia, Sweden, Denmark, Baden and the Dutch Land.They all had the same fear as us, so we simply united. There were many consultations, because all these countries had to agree, the main reason was because—!'

'They are all Protestant!' she guessed brightly.

'Very good!' he praised. He opened his mouth to continue, but she beat him to it.

'France favours the pretender, James the Third as he is called, because she is a Catholic country. Correct?

He laughed. 'Very much so! There has been great bitterness in the House of Commons between the Tories and the Whigs. Walpole is a Whig!'

'How did you get involved in all this? I simply don't understand that at all!'

'Through William of course,' he told her heavily. 'He had contacts, old friends, and I think William was in his cups one day, and started complaining about the country. One thing led to one another, and, before you know it, I was dragged in, because I have some flair for languages, and my French is pretty good. The powers that be wanted a small number of fit, educated, well-trained men with languages for espionage. Men who would kill for their country without hesitation.'

Anne's face became serious. 'Have you?'

'Three times,' he admitted soberly. 'It was either them or me.

She gazed at him coolly. 'I would have done the same then. just like poor William,' she added in a low voice.

He wished she had not mentioned William in that tone as the wound in his heart reopened again. He swallowed heavily and prepared to continue his story.

'At first, I was just a simple courier. Taking messages from here to there. Once I had proved my worth and trust, I branched out, so to speak. Especially as the Whig party were deeply worried.'

'Why them?'

'The war had started to bleed us dry. Trade was at a virtual standstill, and an island like ours cannot survive without commercial trade.The Whigs began to say the war should end with a suitable treaty, beneficial to us of course,' and he grinned wolfishly over at her. 'Negotiations have been going on for some time too!'

The jigsaw of the picture had started to fit

together in her mind. She understood quite a lot, although there were still some gaps to be filled in.

'You have been in the thick of it on the continent too?' she said in a low voice.

He was startled. 'How did you guess that?'

Her eyes twinkled. 'Luck and observation! Remember *that* day, when I saw a very exhausted horse in the stables being fed hot mash. He had recently been shod yet his shoes were thin at the toe clip, and there was also sand on the instep of your boots!'

Richard threw back his head and bellowed with laughter. 'I think you should be doing this job—not me!' he praised, amazed at her astute observations.

'So what was in that valise, which Gaultier so treasured and for which William died?'

His expression became grim. 'A complete list of all the Jacobite sympathisers in this country who will rise up and fight for the Pretender. We have a good idea of some of them, but it is vital that we know every name of the enemy in our midst, because the new treaty has been arranged. That's for what William died and the papers here in my shirt will reach the proper hands. As soon as I get back to London. I will have to deposit you and pass on this list. And till I do that I will not feel I have kept faith with William. I will not have it that he died for nothing!' he said harshly.

Anne nodded, affected by his explanation.

225

William had been true, loyal and a very brave Englishman. How many people would ever know? Who would appreciate his ultimate sacrifice? What honours were there for men who gave their lives in secret for England's glory? She suspected only anonymity would be his reward. 'Not with me!' she told herself. She would keep alive his memory for the rest of her life. It hit her then the extreme danger of Richard's position. She quailed inwardly. Somebody, somewhere, sometime was going to be on the hunt for revenge.

He was surprised at her silence and studied her carefully. Thoughts, ideas and realisations were obviously hurtling through her mind but why the sharp blush of colour and downcast look? What had he said to upset her? He opened his mouth to speak, but she forestalled him, turned to face him, her face stiff.

'You were quite right!' she stated firmly.

Now, it was his turn to be baffled. Did she mean his duty to England? He looked at her anxious and worried.

'To threaten to shoot Night!' she said with firm honesty. 'I was wrong, Richard!'

It was his heart's turn to glow with love and pride. Her admission took guts. 'That's ancient history now,' and he smiled his pride at her.

They beamed at each other and savoured mutual pleasure. He had a wild, crazy yearning to stop the horses, lift her down and make love. She read his mind and understood the depth of his feeling for her. He reached out, and his right hand took her left one and they rode in silence for a little while like that, until both horses began to jiggle fretfully. Each knew its rider had stopped concentrating, and his horse tried a crafty little buck.

'We have to let them out soon,' he commented as he brought his horse back under control again. 'Where was I? Oh yes! Louis was slow to co-operate, but he has finally agreed that the Spanish empire must be split up once and for all. His grandson is going to be accepted as King Philip V of Spain and he will take the West Indies. The Spanish Netherlands and land in the north of Italy goes to the Hapsburgs' Empire. The Dutch will get what they want, which is the line of fortresses, all of which will finish France's ambition to dominate Europe. We will emerge the greatest power because we take Novia Scotia and Newfoundland from France, and Gibraltar and Minorca from Spain, which will combine to make us a mighty commercial nation.'

'What about the Pretender?'

'We do still have a bit of a problem there,' he agreed slowly. 'After a lot of smooth talking and considerable heart-searching Louis has agreed to accept a Protestant line of succession through the Electress Sophia. When Queen Anne dies, which could be any time, our next monarch will be George the

First from Hanover and Hanover favours the Whig party!'

Anne considered this very carefully. 'If you say the Tories preferred the Jacobites might there still not been trouble?'

He grinned at her acuity. 'It will certainly mean a clash in the House of Commons but this is where Walpole enters the story. He is the Whig leader and will shortly be released from the tower to become the leader of Parliament. He will, in effect, become our first Prime Minister with a cabinet to assist him.'

'*What* about these Jacobites though?' she persisted.

He threw her one of his wolfish grins. 'Now we have a detailed list of all their names, we can make life very difficult for them!'

Now she understood why Gaultier had been so desperate to retain his valise. She also finally understood the true, desperate meaning behind William's death. It had been for England. The land he loved so dearly. She had only known him for a short while but his character had stamped its mark on her. She would also stop at nothing to carry out his puzzling last wish. Then something else occurred to her.

'How did you even know Gaultier had this list?'

Richard smiled and shook his head. 'Don't forget my faithful and regular trips to all the coffee houses. Even a clever man like him could not memorise all those names and addresses. We realised this. They had to be written down available for the Pretender, because without it he was hamstrung. He could not, dare not, make a plan let alone move. It was then a case of anticipating where and when Gaultier would make his move back to France. He will be in hiding with sympathisers, right now, until they can smuggle him back. I expect he loathes me as much as I detest him!'

'Mr Wild's organisation?' she wanted to know next.

'Wild hates the Jacobites and has always cooperated with us for the right price, and we have always had gold available. Wild is uniquely placed to pick up information far and wide. I was never a day-to-day highwayman. It was basically a cover to roam far and wide, though I did my share. So I could get to Wild freely without comment by anyone. I don't think I was very good at it,' he mused to himself.

Anne's mind moved backwards in time. He obviously had some financial reward and deposited this with his man in Yate. She suspected, one day he would go back there to claim it all. How strange that she was only here now, because she had decided to run from the farm and sleep in the copse that night.

'What if Mr Wild talks?'

He chuckled. 'And kill the goose, which lays

such lovely golden eggs? Not him! He likes gold too much!'

'I saw him once, when walking with Katie. He seemed a nice, distinguished gentleman. A real sweetie!'

'What! Him?' he exclaimed. 'He is as much a sweetie as a viper!'

She decided not to argue the toss on this point. He must know better than her, yet, reflecting back, Mr Wild *had* seemed polite and affable. She gave a tiny shake to her head. Nothing was ever what it seemed!'

'When will the war end?'

'The Treaty of Utrecht will be signed next year, and we should be at peace, subject to the Pretender's commonsense and Bolingbroke!'

She remembered the name from her eavesdropping. 'And who, pray tell me, is he?'

'He is a peer, who turned against the Protestants to join with the Pretender. He was considered highly dangerous, but I think he will have been neutralised now we have this list,' he told her and tapped his chest where the precious papers rested inside his shirt, secure and hidden.

'Where does that leave you, Richard?'

'Me?' he said thoughtfully. 'Hopefully, out of a job with any luck! Intelligence agents do not need to be thick on the ground in peacetime. I believe I am coming to the end of my double life. We can look forward to a peaceful life in the near future. I think I can safely promise that!'

Peace for him! He had obviously lived with danger at his shoulder for a great time. He would find it easier to settle down as a civilian, with a new wife, a new home in a new district.

'If Walpole has been in the tower all this time, but is still the leader of the Whig party how on earth have you managed to get information to him?'

He threw back his head, with gusts of laughter. 'Simple!' he said. 'Walpole's imprisonment on that false corruption charge changed him into a martyr. All the leading Whigs have visited him in prison including myself. He has been held in such high regard he has been re-elected by his constituency. The House of Commons tried to quash the result but there were such an uproar they had to back down. It has been child's play. Walpole has had regular visits from many people. Myself and others in my work. Poets, writers, and all of his friends. We have all gone in and out just when it suited us. The Tory party made a very grave error, putting Walpole in the tower; the same as the Whigs did with Sacheverell.'

'Will a Jacobite come after you because you bested Gaultier?' she asked anxiously.

He understood her concern and fear and formed a small lie to placate her. 'No! I have nothing to fear. It's all part and parcel of the game of espionage. Win some, lose some. Me and Gaultier were opponents, opposite sides. We certainly respected each other. And William would not want a witch hunt. It was simply business!'

He looked ahead and pointed. 'That's enough for talking for now. These horses are itching to gallop. There's a good inn not faraway so let's ride!'

TWELVE,

Anne ate mechanically. Long afterwards she could not have said what the meal was except it was hot and filled her stomach. All she could do was think. Her mind buzzed with his story as she kept going back over details to make sure she had assembled his facts correctly. Then her mind moved on a stage. What would happen when they returned to London without William? How are earth could his murder be explained satisfactorily without Richard's work being disclosed?

Secrecy was of paramount importance, that was obvious. Another worry touched her next. It was all very well for him to dismiss the Abbé Gaultier, as no longer any threat but what about other people who had Jacobite sympathies? The Abbé might accept what had happened with equanimity, but there was no guarantee about possible future activities from others. Richard would have to be protected, but how? She puzzled at this knotty problem, attacking it from all angles, when gradually an idea started. She studied it while she ate, working backwards and forwards over every foreseeable permutation before acknowledging it was the only hope to protect him. How would he react to the idea though? She knew instantly that he would revolt out of pride and male conceit. She would have to exude tact and diplomacy, and only use bluntness as an extreme, final measure.

He too was engrossed, though conscious all the time of those around him in the crowded inn. His ears constantly scanned adjoining conversations, sifting and sorting through what he could overhear, though he learnt nothing of value or import. He flashed her a look or two signalling caution as they had chosen to eat in the communal dining room. He thought he understood her meditation.The story he had related was enough to astound anyone, yet she could take it all in her stride. Dear God! How he loved his spirited girl! She bewitched and fascinated him, and he lowered his head to avert the hot glow that he knew was in his eyes. A few more loose ends to tie up, and they should soon be free to marry.

When they had eaten to satisfaction, he paid, took her arm and led her outside to where the horses had been readied. They had decided against staying overnight. It was more important to get back with the news of William's death. Once mounted, they cantered for a short while, then pulled back to a walk, so they could converse. She was still involved in complicated thinking which, he sensed, was going to come out in the open any second. He waited patiently, feeling only a little tension.

'If we are going to marry there is something we have to do,' Anne started slowly. She looked at him tenderly. 'I realise that William was always there to protect your back whenever he could. His death means you are vulnerable to a certain extent. You could announce our betrothal as soon as is decent, which will indicate there will be another pair of eyes watching out for you. All right! You said Gaultier would not harm you now, but he may have friends who think differently. You must have made enemies yourself through your work, that stands to reason.'

'Go on!' he encouraged, fascinated with her reasoning powers. Much of what she had deduced was very true but he had no intention of commenting. Indeed he was not all that pleased she had worked it out for herself. There was a set, grim look of determination on her face, which bothered him.

'Espionage seems a very complicated occupation so why don't we turn this to our advantage?' she asked.

He frowned, then completely baffled. 'You

have lost me!'

'If anyone should come looking for you with an ulterior motive they would obviously commence a search in London before spreading the net wider. If you agree, we can eventually have a country life that might be reasonably easy to cope with, because country people are very inquisitive. They miss nothing at all, because they have little else to occupy their minds. If one solitary stranger had shown his nose in my old village everyone would have known in a matter of minutes, because one can't beat country tongues for wagging. After all, a danger that is known is surely a danger that is halved?'

He considered and admired her logic, knowing it was pretty near faultless, but piqued because she had thought of it first. He had to smile, though, because he sensed she had not yet reached her grand climax.

'So?'

Anne took a deep breath. 'Who has the best organisation in London and the provinces for obtaining information?'

His jaw dropped, and he was speechless from a few seconds. 'Wild!' He shook his head violently.

'Why not?' Anne argued. 'He is the perfectly placed person and you say he favours the Whig cause!'

He fell silent and turned it over dubiously. 'No!' he grunted flatly.

'He is also greedy for gold!' Anne pointed out cunningly.

'But—!'

'There are no buts! Mr Wild's organisation is perfect for our use and look how far you say it extends. He could offer us perfect protection, no matter where we might choose to live!'

'I've never heard of anything so crazy!' he grumbled.

'Can you think of a better idea?' she challenged softly. She fell silent, and she guessed he was mentally trying to pull the idea to pieces. He must agree before she could suggest the second part of her idea. She could only hope he would not be too mulish or implacable.

Richard did indeed know how far Wild's tentacles spread. Her idea had great merit, and he wished William were around to advise. 'Your idea is so crazy it might just be the answer. If I can get him to agree!'

Anne knew this was it. She shook her end firmly. 'Not you! Me!

'What!' he shouted, and halted his horse with disbelief. 'That's utter rubbish!'

'Commonsense more like!' Anne retorted acidly.

'Definitely not!'

'Yes, Richard! It will never work if you go to him, but he would be intrigued with me!'

'I said no!'

'And I say yes!' she shot back, his obstinacy and masculine pride raising her temper. How could he be so obtuse? Why could not he understand? After all, they were talking about her life now as well as his. If they married he must understand she was no compliant female. She had her own opinions, motives and actions. More to the point, she was not just a chattel.

She glared at him and saw obstinacy on his face, as well as a rising temper. Her heart sank for a few seconds, then rose in a burst of resentment. Neither would back down. She set her jaw, as her inner self argued she must start off as she intended to go on.

Her suggestion had stunned him and now he saw the wilful look on her face. He knew this was another kind of crossroads. He must enforce his masculine authority from the beginning.

'A wife's duty is to obey her husband!' he snapped coldly.

Anne's eyes blazed. 'I'm not your wife. I am single. And I will not be owned body and soul!'

They glowered at each other, both struggling not to lose their tempers, but not quite sure how to resolve the situation.

'I will not marry you, Richard, to become a new widow!'

The fact she was right pushed his temper higher. 'And I don't hide behind petticoats!' he rasped.

' And neither do I choose to wear widow's weeds!' she shouted back at him.

'I won't consider it!' he barked, ending the matter.

Anne held her breath. He had forced her hand. She had only one weapon left, and her heart ached to use it but she knew she must. 'You will—if you really want to marry me!' she threatened.

Now, it was out in the open, and he blanched at her words. They hurt and frightened him, but he had no intention of submitting to such blackmail.

'You are the most opinionated, pig-headed female I've ever met!' he bellowed at her. 'And no one threatens me—especially a girl!'

'You have the mentality of a three-year-old!' she screeched back at him, tears hovering at his behaviour. How could he behave like this? When she was only thinking of his safety.

He glared over at her. Would she be a virago of a nagging wife? 'You will not set foot near that man!'

'I'll do just as I like because you don't own me!' Anne screamed from temper and frustration.

'That's it! Throw a tantrum! Look how your voice is upsetting that mare!'

'It's your knuckleheaded stupidity!'

Night had indeed started to dither at their raised voices and his horse copied as horses will. Anne made one of her snap decisions.

238

She rammed with her heels and relaxed the reins. Night bolted forward, grabbing her bit with glee. She unleashed herself in her outstanding gallop.

'Come back, you little—!'

'Come and get me!' she screamed.

How she hated him. She wished she had never met him. He was odious, insufferable, dogmatic and bossy, just for starters. How could she think of chaining herself to him for life? She had lost her wits. She was mad!

Night bolted at a pace that made Anne catch her breath with a flash of anxiety. She bent low over the sliding shoulders and worked with her hands, and her eyebrows shot upwards. The mare had indeed been affected. The bit was firm between her teeth, and she was out of control.

'Oh! You too!' Anne cried with exasperation. 'Well, if you feel like that, then get on with it!' and she dug with her heels in frustration and slammed her knees extra tight against the saddle flaps, making sure she was centrally balanced. She had enough caution left to know that if the mare stumbled at this crazy pace she would come off and be badly hurt. She had no fear. Instead, wild exhilaration filled her. This was splendid fun again.

The land flowed ahead, dipping up and down in gentle slopes. When she looked down, the mare's hooves were a simple blur of dark.

The ears were back with indignation at being heeled a second time. Her black mane whipped from side to side as her powerful shoulders slid smoothly under the satin skin, while her feet devoured the ground.

Anne was intoxicated. 'Go on, my beauty!' she screamed with joy. 'Faster! Faster!'

Night had no intention of doing anything else. Anne screeched once more, and worked her wrists, sending impulses down the reins. She fell silent with awe but was secure, though tears cascaded down her cheeks from their row. How long would the mare sustain this pace?

Night started to burn herself out and come back to the bit and Anne felt this and worked with her hands as the mare gave back her lower jaw. She ducked her head and slowed her pace to a very moderate canter to become one with her rider again.

Richard finally caught up on a lathered brown horse. Although fast in his own right, his horse did not have the legs of the black mare and the brown's ears were back in temper at being left behind. His tail switched angrily as he passaged sideways, stiff-legged, every muscle outraged, but responsive to the bit.

'You are *mad!*' Richard bellowed at her, his face tight and white with fear. He had died a thousand deaths in her insane career at that speed across unknown ground, which might have held coney holes. All vestiges of their row had been wiped out, fear strangled his heart. If anything should have happened to her—he had quailed, understanding at last his deep love for this crazy girl. It had finally hit him if he really wanted her he had to take her as she was. He would never mould her to his preconceived ideas of matrimonial gentility. In many ways, she was a law under herself, and probably could not help her reactions.

Anne walked the mare and studiously ignored him, staring through Night's twitching ears. She was secretly amused to realise he could never have caught her, despite the fact he considered himself brilliantly mounted. She felt a smug satisfaction in putting him in his place, although her heart ached at their ridiculous row. Where did this leave matters between them? Could she ever hope to find a satisfactory relationship with him if he would oppose everything she suggested? Her heart ached when she knew she could not back down.

Her silence made his temper rise again. 'Don't start that!' he shouted, wanting her to look at him, say something, anything just as long as she acknowledged his presence.

Anne continued to study the landscape ahead, oblivious to his very presence. The sun was hot now, and she sweated freely. To one side, some small cottages had appeared and a tiny hamlet. Just ahead, she could make out a vague something in the sky and guessed this must be the smoke from London's cooking fires. She estimated they still had some miles to ride and wondered what he would do next. She kept the mare under control, quite ready to take off again if necessary.

'Anne!' he bellowed with frustration, then gave a great sigh. He must change his tactics. No one bullied Anne Howard. My God! His heart swelled as he admired the way in which she rode—stiff-backed, cool and collected, studiously ignoring his very existence. 'Hey, you over there! It's me—remember?' he called, and thought he saw a lip twitch. It was then a grin slid on his own face as he gave a tiny shake to his head. 'Do you know, we've just had another row?'

Anne's face broke as a giggle arose. She turned and looked mischievously at him and her eyes twinkled at his discomfort. 'Yes!' she agreed. 'Do you think we'll do it often?' she teased, her good humour returning now she had satisfactorily made her point.

He shook his head and moved his shoulders, and considered carefully, then gave a chuckle of irony. 'I think so, but please do let me win one now and again for the sake of my male ego!' he told her, and struck an exaggerated pose of masculine hurt.

Anne burst into a gale of laughter. He looked slightly ridiculous, wearing a forced, injured look. Dear Richard! How wonderful he was! How stupid she had been to think bad thoughts about him. Obviously he only had her best interests at heart but, typically male, he had gone out of his way to object, wearing giant boots on both feet. Didn't men know what finesse meant?

'At least life is not going to be dull with you!' he quipped dryly.

'Correct!' Anne dimpled engagingly.

'You little witch! You scared the living daylights out of me at that speed. Don't ever do it again for the sake of my heart!' he rebuked gently.

Anne giggled once more. 'Did you just see how Night went?'

'Yes, I did!' he replied tartly. 'I think you are right. I don't have much between my ears to let you take ownership of such a beast!'

They fell silent as they weighed each other up, his face serious once more. Anne's look slightly challenging.

'Well?'

'I still think you are insane, but all right, try it. I can't think of a better idea, but I don't understand why you and not me?'

Anne felt a flood of relief that he was being sensible again. 'I think if a man tries to see him for a simple talk, Mr Wild would be suspicious and decline whereas a female will intrigue him!'

'Oh, very well. Have it your own way, and I shall be in the background,' he told her sternly.

'With loaded pistols as well. Now we have other matters to discuss,' and his voice became worried.

'William's death!'

'Have you any thoughts?' he asked in a low voice as he had already guessed her fertile brain must have worked out some logical plan.

Anne nodded. 'The main trouble is going to be with Jenny,' she began. 'She misses nothing, so our story must be foolproof. How is it I am alive, while William is dead? How did I get these boy's clothes? How did you appear upon the scene so we are able to return together? I think the best thing is to give a very much watered-down version of the truth.'

'What do you mean?'

Anne collected her thoughts together carefully. 'The coach was attacked by a mysterious highwayman. The coachman and guard were made to flee, so there is no evidence from them. The third and only other passenger was able to escape, and his identity and fate are unknown. I was left alone in the coach, and William had been shot dead. I fled in panic. I wondered lost and frightened. You heard about it because you happened to be in the area, taking my black mare to the stallion for service. She's not on heat but it is hardly likely Jenny will know this as I gather her horsy knowledge is non-existent. In trying to help find the highwayman you bumped into me and rescued me. My clothes were all

244

bloody and all you could get was this boy's attire. Dan and Joe will both know the mare was not in season so you'll have to say you made a mistake. I doubt they'll query this, because they will be too shocked learning about William,' and she looked anxiously at him to see what he thought.

He turned it over in his mind, hunting for flaws, which could trip them both up. 'I think it is quite brilliant!'

She gave a sigh of relief. 'There is another point. This news is all going to reach Mr Wild very quickly if you say his organisation is so good. He will surely want to know about this highwayman, and I think he is the one man who is told the complete truth—by me—not you!'

He had to admit this was another very valid point. As usual, she had gone straight to the core of the subject in a way that aroused his admiration. Between himself and Wild there had always been a natural coolness edging towards antagonism. Only the fact that their political beliefs were identical had enabled the two of them to work together. Even then, both had wished to keep any necessary meetings as infrequent as possible.

'There is one point that may have escaped you. Make it crystal clear to Wild that I pay for his services. It is pure business; nothing more, nothing less!'

Anne nodded. This was the point that had

escaped her. 'What if he keeps written records of all his business transactions? It would mean if he went down, he would drag us with him?'

He nodded. 'Smart thinking, but I have a pretty shrewd idea for anything personal, details will only be carried in his mind. He is pretty clever, and it is true you have the benefit of your gender. He will be softer with you than with any man. However, just to cover our backs, once I have deposited these papers, I intend to write everything down that has happened. I shall make two copies. One will go to a lawyer I know. The second will be deposited with Walpole's secretary—after Walpole has read it! If you think fit, when you see him, you can mention this before you leave although, knowing Wild, he will have guessed!'

'What a marvellous idea. One final point, which might be beneficial, is that I should see him as your official betrothed.This gives extra weight to my visit and my request for help.'

For a while they rode into silence, though Anne's conscience gave the odd twinge or two. Was this the right time to mention the left-handed swordsman? Now she had the whole story from Richard and the precautions they intended to take, surely it was better to keep quiet for the time being at least. He had enough on his mind without her adding to it unnecessarily.

The return to the house was going to be dreadful. It would be even worse going through William's possessions to find his secretive letter, and then to have to make some kind of awesome decision.

'Won't be long now!' he told her unnecessarily because they had moved into a more built-up area with people walking and riding, jostling their two horses who were now very tired.

Anne recognised where they were, and her heart started to thump with anxiety. Swiftly she ran over the story they had fabricated; it must ring true.The danger was going to come from Jenny. Dan and Joe would believe exactly what they were told. Katie would also accept it at horrified face value. Why then did she feel a little prickle down the nape of her neck concerning Jenny? She had a vague, quite horrible feeling, there were some factor for which, through ignorance, they had not allowed. Rack her brains as she might, she could not see any stumbling block.

He rode in stoical silence sick to his guts. It was going to take the most enormous power of will to ride into the stable yard, and know that William would not appear. It was going to be agony to be here without him, and the sooner they could both get away from London the better. He did not think he would wish to see the capital ever again.

The horses knew where they were and increased their walk, anxious to get back to their familiar stalls, where they knew they would find oats, hay and fresh water. They clattered into the yard and the horses halted, stretching their necks as Dan and Joe appeared.

Richard and Anne dismounted, weary themselves. 'See to these horses and make much of them,' Richard ordered. 'And get another ready for me at once.'

The two stablemen hastened to obey, puzzled not to see William but not thinking much of it. Richard threw Anne a worried look and turned to the house with her following.

'Courage! Remember our story!' he whispered as he took her arm. They went in through the usual back door and Jenny looked up startled from where she was making pastry on the deal table.

'Master!' she cried with delight, then her eyes opened with shock at Anne's dress. 'Those are boy's clothes!' she gasped with amazement.

Anne breathed deeply because now must begin the lies and duplicity. Jenny looked from one of their grim faces to the other. 'What is it?' she asked nervously.

Richard knew there was only one way to give such news. He was blunt. 'William is dead!'

Jenny's draw dropped with disbelief, her mind not able to assimilate the statement right away. Very slowly her eyes glazed over as she stared at him, then they slid to Anne and registered unbearable sadness. Jenny stood frozen in time, starting to breathe in shallow, little gasps as her expression altered to one of total horror.

Anne stared back as ice slid down her spine. A dull, sick feeling rose in her stomach as realisation hit her with awful clarity. This was it! The X factor for which they had been unable to plan or calculate. How obtuse they had been. She wished that Richard would look at her so she could flash some kind of warning but he continued to stand there, flat-footed, not quite knowing what to do next.

'Dead?' Jenny croaked.

Anne knew her suspicion was correct, and she stifled a groan. How blind she had been! She listened as Richard continued.

'It's terrible news!' Richard said slowly. 'And it is a long story. I can only give you brief details now, because I have to go to see the coroner.'

Richard carefully related their cooked-up story but kept the details brief. He was fidgeting, almost desperate to get his papers to Walpole.

'So you see, that is what happened. Mistress Anne, can go over the story again with you and I shall be back later to answer any more questions you have—' and he spun on his toes, anxious to be on his way to the tower.

Jenny was fixed to the spot as if carved from stone. Anne moved to a small cupboard where she had seen before a small flask of strong brandy kept. She found it and poured a heavy drink, which she handed to Jenny. 'Get this down!' she encouraged in a gentle voice.

Jenny sank on one of the kitchen stools and obeyed like a child. Anne felt for her and did not quite know what to do next.

'Dead?' Jenny asked again. 'My William! How I loved him!' and she gave a wail of pure misery.

Anne dragged a stool alongside and put her arm around the sobbing woman. Jenny's tears flowed, then turned to hiccups. Katie appeared wide-eyed with astonishment but with a nudge of her head Anne gestured her away. Her mind worked at top speed. How could this affect their plans? Jenny actually knew nothing at all but she would certainly talk. Even when they moved, her loose tongue could be dangerous if anyone specific was after Richard. Which meant Jenny must also be moved, to a far part of the country, in the opposite direction to where Richard intended they would live.

'And he never once cast eyes at me,' and now Jenny wailed pitifully. Katie appeared once more, this time with Mary Bates.

Anne beckoned them. 'Do not leave her.' With a quick little word she gave a brief explanation. 'I must catch the master!' she added urgently.

'He rode out a few minutes ago, ma'am!'

Katie told her. Anne bit her lip. What should she do for the best? Then she realised there was nothing she could do. With a heavy heart, and added worries, she climbed the stairs to her room. She looked at the very far door, which was that for William's room. She could not go to it now. She had no idea how long Richard would be away and she was in no state of mind to start prodding and prying into the possessions that had made a man's life. Tomorrow was another day.

THIRTEEN

It took a number of days before she could pluck up the courage to head for William's room. She saw little of Richard at the moment. He was in and out all the time but gave her a thumbs-up to indicate the precious papers were with Walpole. Politics, she thought. She decided they were not for her. They were far too involved, complicated and convoluted for someone with her straightforward nature. And, as for kings and queens, she knew deep down that she was totally disinterested in them. They could have the Crown, and all the rich trappings that went with the monarchy. It seemed to her a humble country life was far superior for the state of a person's nerves.

She opened the door and went into

William's room. It was large and airy with a bed, wardrobe, drawers and one rather rickety chair. She felt a lump stick in the centre of the throat, but taking a deep breath, she started a search.

She was methodical. William's possessions were sparse, pitifully so, she thought as she piled them on the bed. She almost felt like a trespasser as she began to go through them, item by item. They were so few. She meticulously hunted in every pocket, and even felt the lining of his spare coat. At the bottom of one drawer were spare shirts, and underneath a heavy, very old pistol. She eyed it. When had this last been fired in anger? It was a cumbersome weapon, with an old-fashioned look about it.

Richard had given her a wooden box, and now she fetched it into the room and began to pack, but for the second time examining each item in depth. When she had finished, she closed the lid, sat on the box and eyed the room again. She studied the floorboards, then paced the room carefully, but none had been lifted, and neither were any loose. She turned her attention to the mattress and went over it, inch by inch. But again, she drew a blank. The rickety chair was the next item demanding attention. Sliding her hands down deep into the seat underneath and around the back, she searched but still no letter.

Feeling very baffled she sat on the box again

and went back over William's last few words. A letter! A very important letter which she was to read, but only disclose to Richard when she thought fit. But there was no letter, yet William was not the type to wander in his mind even when dying.

She racked her brains and studied the ceiling laths, but it was obvious they had not been moved in years. 'Where is it, William?' she whispered with frustration.

Finally, with shoulders bowed and shaking her head, she had to give up the search. Was it possible William had deposited the letter with someone else, like a lawyer but, if so, how could she find out? Should she tell Richard? She hesitated doubtfully. He was still stricken with grief and beset with problems. There was the inquest to come, and William's funeral, the plans for them to move, to say nothing of the termination of his secretive work. It would be grossly unfair to add to his burdens.

'I can't say a word,' she whispered and aloud to herself, 'I can't even mention that maniac of a left-handed swordsman.' Yet William said Richard might be in danger, but he had no proof. Only this letter. 'What does it all mean?' she groaned, hands clasped before her breasts.

She stood and eyed the wooden box, then with a heavy sigh shook her head. The only sensible thing to do was to take the box with them to wherever their new home was going to be. Perhaps in the near future, when life had settled down, she would go through it again, but with Richard, and tell him everything. With this decision made, she tied the box with a rope, and dragged it nearer to the door. She gave it a kick from frustration. It was a box which had come with Richard and William years ago, he had explained, and would now go with her and Richard—to where?

Anne groaned. When would everything end?

The only ray of light was when Richard gave her a large diamond engagement ring. 'I dare not wear this openly,' she said softly, after he had sneaked into her room one evening. They had not made love since the murder. Somehow it had seemed wrong while an inquest was held over William's death, and then his funeral. There had been Jenny's grief to contend with and the atmosphere in the house had been sombre in the extreme.

Katie was also consumed with anxiety at the general situation until Anne took her to one side and explained the general plan to move, all of which had to be kept secret for the time being.

Anne had been perplexed when Katie did not display the joy Anne had expected. 'What is it?' she asked with concern.

Katie had blushed scarlet, then looked Anne straight in the eyes for the first time ever. 'It's Dan!' she explained. 'I'm walking out with him. And I like him very much!' she confided.

Anne was relieved it was no additional problem. She almost smiled, but managed to restrain herself on a subject that was obviously dear to the little maid's heart.

'I'm sure the master will wish to take Dan with us to look after our horses. I don't think he'll take Joe though. He's a bit too young and erratic. Also, he's a city boy through and through. Now I have to go out tomorrow morning to see someone and the master wants you to escort me. Will you?'

Katie beamed, her mind completely at rest, her problems solved. After all, Anne had spoken! 'Where are we going, ma'am?'

Anne looked around discreetly. There was no one around to overhear. 'I am going to see Mr Wild but no one is ever to know except the master!' she warned.

Katie's eyes opened wide with astonishment. That was the fun of being with Mistress Anne. She did such astonishing and even outrageous things.

'He is expecting me,' Anne continued quietly. 'I sent him a letter and he will be available to me about eleven in the morning. It is not far. We can walk.' She did not add that Richard would be following them and would loiter outside but only for a given time. Now the actual time had arrived he desperately wanted to drop the whole crazy idea but Anne had been adamant. Without another one of their thundering, and quite exhausting rows, he realised she would not yield.

So dressed up as smartly as any lady of the quality and with her ring hidden under her bodice, she and Katie started their walk while a grim-faced Richard paced fifty yards behind. He had two loaded and primed pistols, and his temper was also on a hair spring. She was right in that they did need a shield for their backs for at least a year but he did not like this one bit. The trouble was he could not think of a better idea, and that rankled with him. Anne was correct. Between him and Wild was a barrier which both had only managed to scale through a mutual political interest.

The girls walked demurely, carefully following Richard's street instructions. They finally stopped and studied the building before them. It went up to four storeys in a quiet area that gently exuded wealth and status. Anne turned and nodded to Richard who leaned against another house wall with a casualness which he certainly did not feel.

With some amusement, Anne climbed the stairs, Katie at her heels and the door was opened instantly. A tall man greeted them and indicated two chairs in a smart vestibule. The girls sat, and again Anne had to smother a smile. Whoever the man was, he had never been in service before, and it was very easy to see the pistol's bulge under a coat.

'Now remember, I will be talking to Mr Wild alone. You just stay here, everything will be quite all right!'

Now that she was actually here, Katie was not so certain but she had blind faith in Anne. Why she acted as she did was beyond Katie's reasoning even if she had thought long enough. She also had other more exciting matters on her mind. Anne and the master were leaving London soon for a country life somewhere and she and Dan were going with them. It was all incredibly exciting, so as a chaperone she was totally useless.

A thickset man appeared from a side door, and Anne was forced to stifle another insane desire to giggle. Mr Wild could at least employ house servants who looked the part and not just rough fighters.

She stood and adjusted a crease in her gown. It was a dark green, the colour of water reeds, and she had selected black shoes and a reticule without a hat. Her fairly long hair was tied neatly at the back with a green and black bow.

With some excitement, she entered a large room whose door closed behind her with a solid clunk. There were numerous leather chairs scattered around indiscriminately, and, at the far end, near an open fireplace, was a long table. Behind this was a tall carver chair, while directly facing this was a lesser one.

As she walked forward, Anne received the

impression the furniture had been placed to put any visitor at a psychological disadvantage.

The figure behind the table rose instantly, and she recognised him but now he was very different. In the street that day he had come across as a benign, old gentleman. Not here. It was the alteration between the wild animal safe behind bars, and that on the loose, ready to rampage with tooth and claw.

For the first time a tiny chill slid down her spine. Was Richard correct, after all? She felt narrow, cold eyes rest upon her as she walked the length of the long room under a silent, shrewd and penetrating scrutiny. He was dressed in dark clothing, which could have been black or a heavy grey. It was difficult for Anne to ascertain the colour because the room's lighting was subdued. There were two other doors, one on each side of the fireplace, and it crossed her mind to wonder if guards awaited there.

Then she knew she flushed. What was there to be afraid of? She had politely requested an interview and this had been granted by return. If this man was as cold-blooded as Richard had said, he would realise she must have an escort somewhere outside in the immediate vicinity.

Wild waited until his guest had reached the chair and sat, before he lowered himself and calmly studied her. It was rare, to the point of being nearly unknown, for any female to wish to visit him and her request had intrigued him. He had conducted a swift, but thorough investigation and his interest was aroused, though his expression revealed nothing.

Long ago, he had assiduously cultivated a bland mask, which concealed all his thoughts, even when his temper rose high. It was profitless to display an emotion that indicated a winning or losing hand. A neutral expression that bordered on indifference had taken time to acquire and cultivate.

His extensive network of informers was far more widespread than anyone understood because Wild knew that money, in appropriate quantities, could just about buy anything, including silence. Most humans had a price. The skill rose from estimating this, then turning it to personal profit, because gain was what life was about. There was something soothing, fascinating, even mesmeric in gold, something almost sensuous when his hands, with their stubby fingers, played with the yellow coins.

Wealth gave power and power gave all. Without it, a man was nothing, no matter his station in life. It was true titles, rank and breeding opened doors usually denied to him but the power of gold gave him the ability to push them wide open to enter when it suited.

He reviewed what he knew of this girl. It was not all that long ago she had been a raw girl from the country. He had been surprised when Mason installed her in his house and even more astonished, even contemptuous, when the girl had stayed. His amusement had expanded once he had learned of her metamorphic change into one of the quality. Was Mason so hard up for a bed-warmer or was there more to this girl than met the eye? Very gradually, his interest had risen when he had learned of her equestrian ability and the fact she scorned a side-saddle. Initially, this masculine trait had switched his mind on to another track, yet there was apparently nothing lesbian about her.

He saw the girl was a little nervous at his scrutiny, though fighting not to show this. She sat just a shade too stiffly in the chair and a nerve twitched a little on the side of her throat. Were her eyes blue or grey? He was uncertain, but they were narrow as if calculating a column of figures, and they did not flinch from his. He was also perfectly well aware that Mason lurked outside, around the corner, a fact of which he approved.

He was astute enough to have erected a number of insulating layers between those who worked for him and his own person. Only a small handful of carefully selected and tested people ever entered his domain.

'It is rare for me to have the company of a charming, young lady,' he began smoothly to break the silence.

Anne had pondered how to play the

interview. Was guile better than frankness? She had debated long and hard and was still uncertain until he spoke. The aura of power that came from him was like a flood tide, and his words released something inside her.

She gave a tiny little snort, unable to restrain herself. 'That's nice of you to say, Mr Wild, but I am no court beauty, and you don't know whether I'm charming or not!' she said, with her customary bluntness. 'I would like to think I can act and dress as a lady, but not all that long ago I was just a simple cowgirl in an obscure Gloucestershire village. A nothing and a nobody!' Then she threw him one of her impish grins. 'And I'm not much different now underneath all this!' and her right hand rustled her skirt. This man was far too sharp to be taken in by lies.

Wild said nothing, but he was highly amused and settled back in his chair to be entertained. So flattery did not impress her. It would be interesting to find out what did.

'I am here to request your help,' she said soberly and awaited a reaction. When none came she carried on. 'You would of course be paid, because there is no taste in nothing. However, if you cannot or will not give your aid, then say so, here and now, and I'll not waste your time or mine. I will go elsewhere,' she bluffed.

'Are you always so forthright, Madam?' he asked and wondered how long Mason would wait before storming in. He was well aware his personal guards would have no chance at all against a man of Mason's calibre. Yet how could Mason send the girl in to see him? He knew he was suddenly disappointed to have found such a flaw in Mason's character.

Anne gave him a straight look. 'I've had no time for flippancy or false hopes. Neither do I suffer from the vapours. It's hard to shock me. What I want to know is, will you or will you not help?'

'How can I without facts?' he parried.

Anne gestured a little with her right hand and lean forward intently. 'It seems nothing is private in London, and perhaps the gossiping is nearly as bad as that of a small village. I thought, if a person lived in a certain way, with a method usually not acceptable to society in general, it is doubtful if this is really secret.'

Wild stayed silent but waggled a right hand for her to continue. 'Surely if the reward was sufficient, help could be given regarding other information?'

Wild nodded slowly, starting to enjoy himself. This chit of a girl had a good mind, and she was heading towards her climax in a smooth manner.

Anne noticed a tiny something show in his eyes and knew she had his whole interest and attention. She took a deep breath to come out with it.

'Whether that person's business is right or wrong, concerns me not one iota just as long as me and mine are not hurt,' and steel edged her words.

'You talk riddles, young woman,' he chided softly.

'I am talking about personal protection!!'

'For whom?' he shot back at her.

Anne threw him a soft smile. 'I think you have guessed!' she said and lifted her left hand a little. The diamond flashed cold and hot at the same time.

'What exactly do you want?'

'Information!'

'You presume I can provide it?' he purred dangerously.

'Yes!' Anne replied bluntly. 'You and your organisation!'

'What—organisation?' he asked with the first edge of menace in his tone.

Anne did not miss this and she just sat with eyebrows elevated.

'Where do you stand in your opinion of me?' he shot at her, interested to see her reaction.

Anne frowned and gave a tiny shrug. 'I don't know!' she told him, tipping her head a little to one side. 'Some people say you do good, while others say you are a dreadful person.They comment you have a robber gang with goods you ship to the continent from a bulging warehouse.'

Obviously Mason had told her because it was highly unlikely his men would dare. He felt a sharp disappointment that Mason's stock had plummeted in his eyes.

'Men have died from saying that!' he told her in a low voice. 'Who told you? Mason?'

Anne felt chilled at his tone yet, oddly, there was something about him that could not frighten her. She was unable to work out what this was. Yet she knew he would not hurt her. She sat back in her chair, more relaxed at any time since she had entered the house. Suddenly she threw him a grin and was at once a young girl again.

'I would be daft to tell you, wouldn't I?' she replied with a devilish glint in the eyes. 'Personally I am not at all bothered what you do just as long as myself, and the man I plan to marry are safe,' and her voice became serious.

'Richard Mason?'

Anne nodded. 'Will you help us?'

Wild set his lips tight and reflected, letting his eyes range over her face. She certainly was no beauty. Her features were almost a little too square for that yet she carried an air about her which was unusual. Certainly she had a bold spirit, coupled with courage . . .

'Why is it you are here and not Mason? Petticoat hiding?'

Anne laughed. He was going to cooperate; she sensed it. 'That's exactly what Richard said, we had a row about it. I thought you

264

would take more notice, if I came. I doubt you would have seen Richard so quickly if at all—now!' she added meaningfully.

Wild's ears twitched.That was very interesting because Mason did not have a loose tongue.

'Anyhow,' Anne continued freely, 'surely marriage is a partnership. I have been open with you, Mr Wild. I have not tried the usual feminine tricks to gain your attention or interest, have I? I am here to talk about a simple business transaction. We want something for which we will pay and you have the wherewithal to provide that which we require.'

Wild looked away then. Behind the closed doors were his two armed guards. Good men but not tough like Mason. They were totally loyal to him because he paid them very well. And that was all. They had not one ounce of sentiment in them. For a few seconds, he felt a flash of jealousy for Mason. This unusual girl was a priceless gem. If only he had known someone like this years ago instead of perhaps?

'Naturally,' Anne continued blithely, 'we should keep a record of all monies paid to you,' she hinted, following Richard's advice and giving a warning.

Wild bristled slightly then gave a cold smile. 'I could blackmail you!'

Anne nodded quickly and flashed him a grin. 'It wouldn't do you much good though!'

'Why not?' he purred with interest. How clever was Mason deep down?

'Because you bleed like anyone else!' Anne said, her voice low and cold.

For a few seconds he was astounded. The girl dared to threaten him? Or was it Mason speaking through her? He had a shrewd idea it was mutual. He noted how she clutched her reticule. It was large for a girl, and he wondered if it held a pistol. It was likely but would she have the guts to use it? He suddenly knew she would not hesitate. He felt a rising respect.

'I do not care for threats, Madame!' he growled.

'What threats?' Anne asked sweetly, throwing in a dimpled smile for good measure.

'You could vanish here and now, before anyone from the road could break in!'

Anne looked him straight in the eyes, cool and unperturbed. 'And you would make an awful mess, bleeding all over the chair where you sit!' she riposted neatly.

He was staggered at her nerve and effrontery plus the confirmation she did indeed have a pistol. Whether she was an accurate shot would be a mere bagatelle. At this close range even an infant could not miss.

'I'm not sure I care to barter with females. Their place is in the kitchen or bedroom!'

'Stuff and nonsense!' Anne retorted tartly. 'A wife's place is at her husband's side!'

They both glared at the other, but it was Anne who spoke first once more. 'You had a business relationship with Mary Milliner when you left the debtor's prison. You even opened a brothel with her. Why are you so nervous with me, sir?'

He took a huge breath, deeply stung. 'I don't think I care for you or your affairs.'

She had gone too far.

'I'm not exactly clapping my heels with glee about you either!' Anne snapped. This was not going as she had planned. She had overdone the provocation, but who did he think he was to sit there in majestic glory like the Queen herself? 'But I've always understood business can make strange bedfellows.'

She stood, taking care to keep her right hand near the top of her reticule which her left held tightly. He was not going to cooperate, which was a shattering blow but beg, whine and plead she would not. He was quite insufferable. Richard had been correct about him. She was hugely disappointed her brilliant idea had turned into a washout.

'I will think about it!' he said suddenly in a ponderous manner. Anne blinked as fresh hope soared. What could she do now to tip the scales in her favour. She racked her brains.

'Mr Walpole will soon be a power in the land,' she told him carefully. 'You are perfectly well aware of Richard's activities, which means finances are no problem provided they are realistic!' she baited.

'How do you know I would not turn against you?' he asked curiously.

'We don't!' Anne told him honestly. 'But surely only a fool kills the goose laying the golden eggs and you, Mr Wild, are nobody's fool!'

'Continue!' he told her in a more sensible voice. Gold! And his eyes gleamed!

'We leave shortly to start a new life in a house in Gloucestershire in a village called Iron Acton. We can not marry just yet because we are mourning for—' and her voice tailed off. She flashed him a look and realised he knew all about William, which obviously meant he was quite familiar with exactly what had happened and the Jacobite Abbé Gaultier.

'Wise! Understandable!' he said softly.

'Richard will make arrangements to pay you monthly for all or any information you receive and concerning anyone who might inquire about him or whom you think could be a threat to either of us. Once we are established with servants around us, and hounds, we will be secure, because village people miss little. This is the address,' and she handed him a small piece of paper. 'We have tried to cover our tracks by only taking two young members of staff with us and transferring others to distant Norfolk in better, higher paid positions. We will be moving ourselves in a few short days, taking just my maid, and one stable boy.'

He looked down at the address. 'This will be burned later!' and Anne believed him. 'What do you offer for my services?'

Anne threw him a cheeky grin. 'Oh no! Haggling is not my task. I have laid the groundwork. You and Richard can fight that one out between you!'

He threw back his head and laughed, then became serious. 'What dowry do you take to this marriage?'

Anne had not expected such a question. Her face became a little sad, then her jaw jutted. 'Myself, my character, my pride and my loyalty, plus a few gold coins. That is all I have in the world. No money, no family, no breeding. Just me as I stand before you!'

Wild softened . . . 'You love Mason very much?' Then he fell silent before he spoke again. 'I was a husband once. Indeed, I have a son,' and he paused. 'I have not seen him, nor my wife in more years than I care to relate. Way back down the years I lost something. A precious something which has gone forever. Make sure you never lose it. Hang on to that which you hold dear. It can happen so easily,' and he looked down at his hands, for the first time his exterior of hardness broken.

Anne understood in a clairvoyant flash. She was seeing a side of him kept hidden from all other people. She read weariness and sorrow and saw this was not a happy man despite his wealth and power. He stood up and came around to the front of the table to sit on its edge, only feet from her. Bending slowly, he took her right hand and gazed deeply into her eyes. Anne knew she blushed. With great courtesy Wild lifted her hand and touched it lightly with his lips.

'I salute you, madam! I hope Mason fully understands the bargain he is getting!!'

'Oh!' was all Anne could manage, delighted with his gesture, but also a little embarrassed.

'A sealed note to this address will always reach me. Use this seal,' and he handed her one from his pocket. 'It just shows a J and W intertwined. Never let anyone else have possession of it. It is my personal seal, known only to a handful of very trusted people. Any note I send to you will have the same seal. Cleave to your man, Anne Howard. In the future, if you should hear bad about me, as no doubt you will, do not judge me too harshly. Some of us make irreparable mistakes in our young days. We set off on a certain path through circumstances beyond our control, because of inexperience of life itself. Once upon the path it is difficult, if not impossible, to leave it. The path has to be followed even when it leads to the end of a rope.'

He stopped and looked bleakly across his room as the grip on her hand tightened. 'There are times when the path can be very lonely. At least you two will be a pair, which is nature's design. You are wise to leave London. It is going to take much time for this country to settle down again. Even when all hostilities do cease. Gradually though, any enemies Mason might have made will fade away. It is hard work to keep up a blood feud. Any danger to him will be just about immediate and as soon as word reaches me you will be informed.'

As Anne listened and concentrated she felt a wave of kindness come from him. Her heart was touched. Where was the Viper now?

'I doubt I'll die in bed,' he said slowly. 'I expect my end will be violent, but I have to live the only way I know how!'

'Thank you, Jonathan Wild. Whatever I hear about you from others will not change what I think about you here and now,' and standing on tiptoes, she softly kissed his cheek. He took her elbow and escorted her to the door, opened it, and an anxious Katie looked at both of them.

'Wait!' he said sharply, turned and strode back into his room. Anne was perplexed but obeyed. After a short while he was back again and handed her an exquisite brooch. It was as large as her thumb and of a horse moving at the gallop with flying mane and tail. The metal gleamed yellow, and she gasped as she realised it was gold. Small green emeralds made the horse's eyes glow, and it had been moulded with loving care so that speed and power flowed from the horse.

'It's incredible!!' she gasped with awe. 'But is it—?' and she floundered to an embarrassed halt.

He smiled. 'No! It's not stolen! It is something I have had for years, because it belonged to my mother, and how she obtained it I do not know! Wear it for me, will you, as my wedding gift.'

'I will wear it with enormous pride. Pin it on me!' she asked him gently.

He did this, moving carefully, then stood back and beamed his pride. 'If Mason is jealous—too bad! Walk and ride with God, my child, remember all I have told you and think of me sometimes!'

Then he spun on his heels, walked back into his room and shut the door. Anne was stunned into silence. Perhaps nothing had ever touched her quite as much.

'It's gorgeous!' Katie breathed.

Anne was bemused. 'We had better go. The master is around the corner and I don't want him charging in here either!'

The girls walked down the steps just as Richard hove into view, a murderous look on his face. As he saw them he bounded forward.

'Are you all right?'

'Never felt better!' Anne assured him.

'I was just coming in to—!'

'There was no need. He was marvellous and I gave him a kiss before I left!'

'You did—what?' he gasped, then saw the

stunning brooch.

'A wedding gift from him. I have a lot to tell you when we are private but briefly he will cooperate though you can go and do the haggling. Count me out on that one. I still think he is a sweetie and—'

Richard let out a loud snort. His nerves felt frayed. It had taken considerable willpower to stand and wait for what seemed many hours. Now here was his Anne back, safe and sound, but extolling the virtues of a man whom he knew he would never like. And with a valuable piece of jewellery to boot. He shook his head in complete confusion.

Anne saw this and decided it would be prudent to change the conversation. They walked together and Katie dropped back two paces to allow them a degree of privacy.

'What is happening about the Jacobites?' Anne asked casually.

'I don't think they will make much too much trouble now. If they have any sense, they will realise they have shot their bolt. There will be growlings of discontent from certain people, but most certainly, there will not be a King James the Third on the throne. It is definitely going to be King George the First of the Hanoverian dynasty with a guaranteed Protestant succession!'

'You have had a hand in the making of history,' Anne told him with respect.

'And so did William,' he remarked sadly.

FOURTEEN

'Well it doesn't look much right now, but what do you think?' Richard asked anxiously.

Anne stared around. They had ridden down gently, and stayed overnight at an inn but now that she was back in what was her home territory she felt a few qualms. It seemed strange to be within two miles only of Yate, yet a totally different person. She calculated that it was not all that far from here to the few trees under which she had spent that momentous night. It was a lifetime ago.

She knew that when she was thoroughly settled in, she would go riding on Night through the little village and once she was recognised how tongues would wag. This was something which would amuse her enormously.

Dan and Katie had come on ahead, with all their personal heavy goods and were planning to marry right away and move into a cottage nearby, which Richard had bought. Until then Katie lived in a top-floor room while Dan boarded in the actual village. They only had their two riding horses at present so he spent his spare time moving furniture and helping in general.

They walked all over the house and Anne was delighted with it. It stood in solitary isolation well away from the village, yet near enough still to be part of it. There were three huge rooms downstairs, with an enormous kitchen, which had a stone-flagged floor and a tremendous cooking range. Upstairs, there were four big rooms, and the attic had three more. Katie had promptly commandeered the largest attic room for herself, which overlooked open countryside. She was completely fascinated by this, which was all totally new to her.

'I still have a bit more local riding to do,' Richard told her. 'One or two odds and ends to be tidied up and I will then be a gentleman of leisure,' he grinned.

Anne smiled up at him. 'You and your old secrets!' she teased. 'You will be lost without them! What do you plan to do? I can't see you being an idle gentleman of leisure?'

He had already worked that one out. 'I would like to breed fast, riding horses. Eventually have our own stallions here!'

'What a splendid idea!' and she looked at him with admiration. It was also a relief. After such an active and dangerous life, it was imperative Richard had something to do with a degree of stress.

'You have been very good. You haven't asked any awkward questions, and you must be bursting with them! By the end of the week, at the very latest, I should have a bit to tell you which will cause you great amusement and interest.'

Anne smiled. She knew she was consumed with curiosity, because it was in her nature. But she had learned to put a lid on this now. After all, she also had a confession to make. He still had no idea she had eavesdropped on what was a private business conversation, and neither had she ever explained about the weird left-handed swordsman.

'Now, what is on your mind?' he wanted to know, as she had gone serious.

'Girl's thoughts!' she tossed back at him. 'You have your secrets, perhaps I may have some too!'

'Do you indeed!' he replied, knowing perfectly well she did. What these could possibly be he simply had no idea, but his finely honed instinct had never let him down. All along, he had felt she was a party to some information, which concerned him, but which escaped him.

'What do you know that I don't know?' he asked with a little irritation in his voice.

'When you tell me yours, then I'll tell you mine!' she offered in a soft voice.

'That's a bargain!' he said quickly. 'And I'll be holding you to it as well!'

For the next day the four of them worked hard until Dan went to his lodging, and Katie retired to her room, tired out.

'I have to go out for an hour this evening to your old village of Yate. I don't expect to be too long, and when I come back I might be able to give you some interesting information!' and his eyes twinkled with amusement.

Anne studied him with a degree of exasperation. How men liked their secrets! 'Am I allowed to ask who you're going to see?' she wanted to know tartly.

He pretended to consider then laughed. 'Why not? It's old Lady Sarah Penford!!'

'What!' Anne was staggered. 'She saw me the day I left the farm and gave me a gold coin. I still have it!'

Richard closed his eyes for a moment. 'She did—that? How like her! She always was a rebel!'

Anne nodded. 'That's one old lady I'd very much like to meet again. She must be terribly old?'

'She's in her late eighties!'

Anne was staggered 'That old! What an incredible old lady. I bet she has some stories to tell. How I would like to hear them!' she marvelled with awe.

'Tomorrow I'll take you to her!' he promised. 'And now I must get off. I'll head in the direction of Yate first!'

Anne looked out of the window. It was already early evening and would soon be pitch dark, but she suspected he had cat's eyes at night.

After he had gone she mooned around downstairs, wondering whether she did really like the furniture in its current position or not. As she came to the small vestibule, she noticed the letter that had been hand delivered and which she had totally forgotten. She picked it up curiously, not recognising anything until she turned it over and the seal with J W stood out clearly where he had pressed his against the hot sealing wax.

She bit her lip with worry. Her own ring with its private seal was carried in a little leather pouch, attached to her belt, which also held the housekeeping keys

Her heart throbbed as she broke the seal with a fingernail.

'Your old housekeeper now in Norfolk has been questioned regarding your whereabouts and the same here in London. A man has been seeking your new location. I do not know his name, nor his nationality at present. From his speech, English may not be his mother tongue. I will try to get more details for you. I think this man will eventually find your new address, and would suggest you take suitable precautions until I can provide more information. My salutations. J W

Her stomach gave a heave as panic rose. She cursed for not opening the letter earlier, while Richard had been present. She frowned heavily and went back over the cryptic lines, puzzling and pondering. Richard had said Gaultier would never bother to come after him personally, what had been between them was pure business. Was this enquiring stranger also French or a Jacobite sympathiser?

She felt confused and bit her lip She must think coolly and carefully. At least she knew where Richard was. Otherwise, she was alone in the house with just Katie on the third floor. If someone was asking questions it had to relate to Richard's days in London, which meant either his political work or highwayman's activities. She dismissed the latter, because John would have known about that and said.

A little ominous something rose in her mind, which she pushed away. It was ridiculous, but then, her inner self argued, was it? She had a flashing vision of the night she was locked out and trapped in the yard. The soft-footed prowler. The man she had seen in the street. The rider who had followed her. Her heart quailed with indecision.Who on earth could it be but him? Why though? All political decisions had been made and settled. Was he pursing a lone vendetta for some unknown reason? Was he related to someone whom Richard had killed in the past about which she knew nothing at all? Did he suspect she was party to everything? If so, he was hopelessly wrong and had no idea at all, how secretive Richard could be.

She thought about getting Katie, then dismissed that idea. Weapons, she asked herself, where were they? Richard had given her some lessons with the small pistol which had been in her reticule, but she lacked confidence.

Richard never went anywhere without his sword and two pistols. She felt she would like a weapon in her hand even if she couldn't load or use it. But where was there one? She thought rapidly. There was nothing in the house; she would have noticed when they were pulling furniture around. William's old pistol! Now where had they put the box with William's possessions?

She grimaced with annoyance and thought back, then remembered. As they only had two horses in the stables they had put goods in the spare stalls, which were not required immediately. William's box must obviously be piled with the other miscellany.

She looked outside. It was pitch dark now and the moon was only fitful. Great dark clouds scurried across the sky as the wind rose to a bit of a howl and it started to rain quite heavily. She pulled a face, slipped on outdoor shoes, and draped a cloak around her shoulders. Richard had the key to the front door, which was firmly locked. She would unbolt the rear door, run over, find William's box and extricate his heavy old pistol. Even if it couldn't be used it would look good and make her feel an awful lot better.

She looked down at Richard's old breeches, which she wore while working around the house.They were much too large, and she had tucked them up around her waist with a belt. She knew perfectly well she was outlandishly dressed for a female but in their home she didn't care. And neither did Richard.

She swiftly pulled back the two heavy bolts to the back door. She would only be a moment. Outside the wind blustered and the rain squalled slanting viciously so, bending her head, she ran blindly to the stables.There she opened the top and bottom doors and slammed them to and slid over their bolt. Night jumped, a little startled, and uttered an enquiring whinny. The mare was lonely. She was used to horses in all neighbouring stalls and was glad of human company. Anne went up to her, spoke soothingly and stroked her neck so gradually the mare settled down again and carried on eating her hay.

Anne went into all the empty stalls and finally spotted William's box under a collection of bridles, reins, rugs, buckets, halters and all the impedimenta that go with keeping horses. With a grunt of satisfaction she unfastened the ropes, lifted the lid and dived down to the bottom, where she remembered she had placed the pistol. All around were sacks and boxes of household goods not immediately wanted and it crossed her mind there was an awful lot of sorting out to do right here.

Although it was now very dark outside her eyes had adjusted and the moon was more obliging as the rain eased a little. She decided though to light a lantern with flint and tinder. It threw only a dim, yellow glow but she hung it up carefully. Lit lanterns which fell in stables were highly dangerous to man and beast with so much combustible material around like straw and hay.

From outside, there was a maelstrom of noise. The wind had risen again. Timbers creaked and groaned, while some of the slates murmured a threat and to one side tree branches clapped. She peered through a cobwebbed window. Overhead dark clouds scurried across the sky as the rain started to lash again.

She regarded the pistol thoughtfully. She held the barrel towards the lantern's glow and frowned. Something appeared to be blocking it and with a fingernail she started to tease it loose. She worked patiently and carefully and was surprised to see a tightly rolled paper appear. At the same instant, her heart started to pound. Was it possible she asked herself? What an ingenious hiding place.

Excitement filled her as she carefully unrolled William's letter. No wonder she hadn't been able to find it before. Anne went over to the lantern, dragged up another part-packed box, sat and started to read.

After only a few lines, she gasped with shock and then as she proceeded her mind whirled. By the end of the letter she was confused, bewildered, touched and near to tears. The blood hammered in her temples, as so much of the past's puzzles became clear at last. Dear God, was she going crazy? She looked at the data on the letter and flinched. It had been written on the evening prior to her and William going on that fatal coach ride. No wonder William had insisted she relate the contents only when she considered the moment opportune. Was *this* the time? Yes, she told herself grimly. Wild's message, and William's letter, confirmed with a vengeance. She bent her head to read the letter for a third time, shaking her head with amazement at some of the sentences.

Dear Richard

This letter is going to curl your hair as well as make you curse. I had always intended to tell you to your face, when our task was finished but events are moving too fast now. Also, I have an uneasy gut instinct, which I do not like. I do not think time is on my side so, here goes. You have left with the two horses, and we will not be able to talk together until we have queered Gaultier's pitch so

I am doing this now, just in case. I will lodge it down the barrel of my old pistol the one you used to play with as a boy. you'll find this in due course.

However, before get down to the nitty-gritty, 1 must warn you, I only found out this morning, after you had departed, and there is little proof just plenty of gossip. It seems there is a man in England, who is a member of a hard-line Jacobite splinter group. Rumour has it he has links with Gaultier, through family and marriage connections. His father is a Scottish Catholic, while his mother is a French one. That makes a pretty bad mixture to put it mildly. I could not find out his name, but there is one way to recognise him. He is left-handed. He has also been seen passing his wineglass over the water tumbler before the royal toast. More fool him, because it is a dead giveaway. I could find out little about him except that he has been flitting in and out of the country for the past few months—but for what? Watch out for him. The fanatic makes the most dangerous enemy of them all. Certainly he will hate you after what we've done for Gaultier, so guard your back if I'm not around, my son.

Because that is who you are. Duly cherished and beloved only son. I wish Jane, your mother, could see how well you've turned out. Who knows, perhaps she does? She died, when you were very small, of a lung sickness, and her death devastated me because I loved her dearly. I went to pieces completely and acted like a fool. I had you to raise all alone so I started to gamble with the dice. Myself and a friend ran up huge debts. There was a fight and he was run through with a sword and died in my arms. I then saw a way to break free. I took his identity— he had no family—and fooled the debtors. Moved and raised you but became your manservant in everyone's eyes, yours included.

That was all a long time ago and only one person ever knew the whole truth who forgave me. I have always kept in touch with that person by carrier pigeon. When your work ends go back to these roots and this person whom you do know. It is of course old Lady Sarah Penford, your great grandmother.

When you returned with Anne, from that area of all places, I was livid with you. I saw the girt had bewitched you and I wanted more than a cowgirl for my son's

285

wife. I was wrong! That girl has backbone with some good blood from somewhere. Marry her—if she will have you! I found out her mother was Emma Howard, a by-blow of Lord Henford. So you see when Anne stood up to both of us, she was following her breeding because there are no wimps or fops in the Henford line.

There is so much more I would like to tell you but no time. Remember I will be proud to have Anne Howard as a daughter.

Your affectionate Father WILLIAM

Anne's shoulders slumped. It was all too hard to assimilate especially about herself. She gave a huge sigh of sadness for herself, Richard and William. She felt tears hover at the tragedy of it all. The pathetic waste. Slowly she rolled up the precious letter and tucked it carefully under her shirt.

She thought about Wild's message and William's information. Her blood chilled. As soon as Richard returned she must tell him all. Suddenly she noticed her mare. She had stopped feeding and stared at the two closed doors, ears pricked alertly. The mare had heard something and was curious in the way of all horses. At the same time, ice slid down her spine.

She held her breath but the only sounds which reached her where those of the wind and the rain. She did not like the mare's curious alertness then she stilled as Night uttered an enquiring nicker. There was another horse somewhere very close by indeed and it would certainly not be Richard's. He would see the lantern's glow and call out his greeting which meant . . . ?

Her blood turned to ice. Only one person would loiter outside, on another horse, in such foul weather. They were still unknown in the region and visitors went to the house, not the stables. She had run over swiftly and caught him unawares. Now he had come back with his horse. For what purpose? To kill, certainly, and Richard would come riding back in all innocence straight into an ambush. She chewed her lip with frustration and rising anger. Just who the hell did this man think he was?

In a flash she knew what she must do and acted as her temper started to sheet high. Moving swiftly, she saddled and bridled her mare, taking pains to ensure the girth was tight. She bent down and gently opened the bolts of the two doors. She carefully doused the lantern, pushed William's pistol down her belt, and mounted silently.

The wind and rain still squalled noisily as, bending from her waist, she grasped both doors and flung them open with a bang. She dug with her heels, ducked her head down against the low beam, pulled the pistol from her belt as Night shot from the stall with alarm.

The mare's shod hooves clattered on the cobbles, sending tiny sparks into the slanting rain. The whole movement was so unexpected he was taken by shock as well as surprise. The mare's black colouring complete with wild girl on her back waving a pistol made him rein back sharply, away from where he had been sheltering against the weather.

Anne added to this devilish scenario by screeching like a mad thing and his frightened horse reared in protest. He had to struggle to retain his seat then girl and mare were gone into the rain-swept night in an awesome black blur.

For a fleeting second Anne's eyes rested on him, seeing him as she had before—grim faced, narrow-eyed and now one pistol in his hand. The pistol barked but the ball went hopelessly wild as his horse dithered with fright. He rammed it into its holster, grabbed the second, spurred his horse back under control and chased.

Anne rode as if mad. She knew exactly where to go but had never been out in such foul weather . . .and within half a dozen strides she was disorientated. Yate must be in that direction she told herself but she recognised nothing. The atrocious weather had changed all. He roared something at her as she urged Night recklessly faster.

Anne realised her mare was quite out of control from shock, the proximity of the chasing horse and the foul weather. She wondered where would Richard be? In a house or on the return journey? She felt frantic to intercept and warn him of the madman at her rear. Night charged forward, quite oblivious to her bit, intent only on going faster and faster even if it was into the teeth of slanting rain.

Anne fought her savagely. A bolting horse over flat ground in daylight was scary but also fun. This insane pace, in the dark and such vile weather, was quite terrifying. For the very first time in her life she was petrified and did not know what to do. If she came off at this pace her neck would break and, at any stride, the mare's hooves could slip and she would be down with Anne underneath, crushed to death.

She wondered exactly where she was. She dared not unbalance herself at this speed by turning to look behind. She wondered also where he was. Her mare had veered off in her crazy bolt. She was sure this was not the turnpike to Yate. She worked with her hands in a violent struggle to regain control but the mare was having none of this.

Then there was an explosive bang at Anne's

rear as he discharged his second pistol. It hit the mare who leapt up in the air in a paroxysm of shock and pain. Anne had no chance. She was flung from the saddle as the mare crashed down on the opposite side.

With the resilience of youth, Anne rolled to her feet then stood a few seconds in total shock. Her mare lay on her side as the rain started to lash down again with ferocity. A cry caught in her throat at Night's death, then self-preservation took over.

She heard his horse coming, snapping its hooves against twigs and light branches blown off by the wind. The rain eased fractionally but it was so dark. She had no idea where she was so turned and plunged through some bushes, hands outstretched to feel obstacles. Could he possibly see her?

If only she knew exactly where she was. Yate was so near but it could been a thousand miles away to her on foot—against him mounted. Her wits started to work. Both of his pistols had been discharged and he could certainly not stop to load and prime them in this weather on the back of a fidgety horse. If only she had some kind of a weapon herself to even out the odds of his greater strength.

She blundered forward a few more paces then stopped to lean against a tree and catch her breath. It had stopped raining again and, looking up, she fancied the clouds were thinning. If only the moon would show a little, then, suddenly, it obliged and she gasped. This was—uncanny. She was at the tiny copse where she had spent her first night and met Richard. She looked around wildly and recognised the same animal trail. A feeble idea entered her head as she heard his horse ponderously crashing towards her.

She darted over the trail and shot behind an obliging shrub then looked around frantically. Her eyes hunted then she saw exactly what she wanted. It was a broken-off piece of tree, about a yard long and fairly straight. Old, dead wood. She picked it up and with snarling teeth waited. Her heart pounded so loud—surely he must hear?

The horse plodded nearer, letting out snorts as it picked up her scent. Suddenly it loomed over her. Less than two feet away. She sprang to her feet and screamed. At the same time she lunged forward with the dead wood. From its eye corner the shocked horse could only see a dripping apparition that then plunged forward with something aimed at its tender genitals. Quite sensibly the horse reared in protest and shock, anxious to protect the most tender part of its body.

The rider had no chance. He was shocked at the girl's attacking action and his mount's natural objection. He did not even sway in the saddle. He was tipped straight from it and . . . relieved of its rider the other horse bolted away from such a frightening place.

Anne leapt forward. As she had guessed he fell on his left side. With a giant stride she was over him and before he could collect his senses she had ripped out the sword on his right-hand side. She had never touched one before but instinct told her what to do—that and her driving will to live. She plunged the sword tip in his chest. It hit a rib, slid off then plunged straight into his heart as she leaned on it. Wild-eyed with rage, fury and fear; teeth bared with natural, female ferocity.

He died instantly and Anne leant back against a sodden, moss-covered tree trunk and stared, almost hypnotised, at what she had done. She panted with exertion and stress but there were no tears. Just boiling hot triumph. Now perhaps they could try to live in peace.

'Anne!' a voice bellowed frantically.

She spun on her toes. 'Richard! Over here!' she screamed, frantic now for his company and comfort.

He crashed towards her on foot, took in the scene in one sweeping glance, then grabbed her in his arms. 'Are you hurt?'

'No! I'm not! He is though! Hurt dead at last!' and there was a touch of hysteria to her voice now. 'I have so much to tell you!'

'Sshh! Sshh!' he soothed. What exactly this was all about he did not know but guessed it was tied in with her secrets from him. Something traumatic had obviously happened and when he first heard the pistol's bark, carried even through the wet air, he had known it had to involve his beloved Anne.

'He killed Night!' she wailed like a little child.

'No, he did not!' he told her quickly and she stopped crying and looked at him, wide-eyed with hope. 'The ball went in to the top part of her neck and through it. We can soon stop the bleeding and see to it.'

'But she went down!'

'So would you from the initial shock!' he told her dryly 'A ball has a big kick to it!'

She rested her sodden and filthy hair on his chest.

'Come now. We'll go home and each tell a story. We'll ride double and lead your mare as she is feeling just a little bit sorry for herself!'

He looked around. She managed a limp smile. 'It's weird.This was where it all started.'

He nodded, recognising it all, and, taking her hand, he led her away from the corpse. The law could deal with that man in the morning. Now, he knew, was the time really to start their life together.

*   *   *

Jonathan Wild did find the sands of time running out. In 1725 he was arrested and committed to Newgate. In May, he went on trial, was found guilty and sentenced to death. In the early hours before his execution, he attempted suicide with laudanum but botched the effort. He was hanged at Tyburn on the morning of 24th May 1725.

Jonathan Wild was perhaps one of the most organised criminals this island has ever known. He put the Great Train Robbers and the Brinks Matt mob in a kindergarten class—and this at a time when there was no police force.

He was also totally ruthless. If any of his men turned against him he had no hesitation in informing on them even if it meant their execution.

A search of the records fails to turn up any information indicating possible assassination attempts, which indicates the fear in which he was held by the criminal element.

Walpole has long been recognised as the first modern Prime Minister with a Cabinet. The Jacobites rumbled and agitated for a few years, with an uprising in 1715, which gave Walpole a bit of trouble but this was simply the last throes of a dying cause.